Izzy's Darkest Desires

Come to Bed

Come to Head

By Sage RelleAnne

Rainbow Publishing House LLC

Book Cover by: Wallflower Designs

Come to Bed

Come to Head

Come to Bed

A Dark Why Choose Romance

Sage RelleAnne

Rainbow Publishing House LLC

Proofread by Anna Lisa Vitale and Ashleigh Voros of Split Leaf Saturdays book editing

First edition 2024.

Introduction

Hi all,

This has gone through several rounds of editing and a round of proofreading. If anything still managed to slip through, please let me know. My email is sagerelleanne@gmail.com

If you have not read anything by me yet, a few things before you buckle into this wild ride.

All of my stories will end in an HEA, but the ride getting there? It will be bumpy. This is book 1 of a duet, it ends on a minor cliffhanger.

I write in both first and third person. This will be pretty consistent among all of my novels. For this one Izzy is in first POV and the men will be in third. Most have loved this, but some have most decidedly **not**.

Please feel free to add me to follow for updates on all my projects.

Now that, that's out of the way, thank you so very kindly for giving my book a read. I greatly appreciate your support!

Okay I promise that's everything (besides the triggers).

VERY IMPORTANT

This book has quite a few trigger warnings.

For an extensive in-depth list please reach out to me at: sagerelleanne@gmail.com

Brief outline of triggers:

Somnophilia & Dormaphilia

CNC

Off page assault

Attempted SA

Death, gore, and murder

Loss of loved ones

Stalking

Excessive alcohol consumption

Explicit sexual content

Acknowledgements

Sorry hubby. I don't think you knew what all marrying me entailed.

Dedication

To all you beautiful people that have looked in a mirror and felt that you weren't enough.

You are.

I promise.

It's the world that isn't.

dorm·a·phil·i·a

a paraphilia characterized by sexual arousal or interest in engaging in sexual activities while asleep or unconscious.

Prologue

Izzy did her best to calm her breathing and fall asleep.

She found it difficult, because she knew when she woke up, it would be to a man. Inside her. Filling her up, fucking her, and fulfilling her darkest desire.

Chapter 1

Izzy

I thought at this point in life I might have a bit more figured out. I did my best to check all of society's boxes, but honestly, it was never sufficient. I wasn't quite beautiful enough. I wasn't quite exciting enough. I just wasn't quite *enough*.

At least that's what Harry said when I caught him dick-deep in another woman's asshole a few weeks ago.

I let out a frustrated sigh, and my coworker mean-mugged me. I returned the look but then smiled at the end.

"How about this weather?" I chirped. My dad wasn't lying when he said I would end up talking more about the weather than anything else.

It was monotonous. Everything was at this point.

My coworker gave me a weird look but then turned back to her computer screen. She was such a good little worker; that's why we hired her.

I refocused my attention to the video on my phone. I was playing it on an endless loop.

Letting air hiss out through my teeth, I witnessed as Harry came inside the poor girl. Thirty seconds really wasn't going to do much for her, and he didn't even touch her clit once. And no lube prior? The whole thing felt like a big yuck.

I needed to stop torturing myself by watching this recording, but I found that any time I grew lonely, it was a sure way to remind myself why being single was the better option.

I glanced over my shoulder to confirm no one else could see what was on the phone's screen. I really didn't need a meeting with HR.

I knew Harry wasn't shit; key in on the camera I installed to catch him in the act. But really? My step-sister? On my birthday? He couldn't be more cliché if he tried.

A throat clearing had me swiveling my desk chair.

"Boss man." I smiled jovially at my best friend and "boss," Oliver. That was one reason this "job" wasn't too bad.

His golden curly hair fell forward in disarray as he creased his brow in annoyance. His large hand reached up to brush it out of his vibrantly ashen blue eyes before dropping it to his side. My gaze traced the movement in a trance, and I slowly followed a path up his suit. His muscles pushed against the fabric, rebelling, and I watched as the material stretched on every exhale before finally resettling on his eyes. They were crinkled in amusement.

Oliver knew he was hot shit. "I told you not to call me that." There was humor in his deep voice.

It did something to my nerves, and I decreed then and there, I needed to get laid. Harry and I hadn't had sex for several months prior to his dick ending up in my step-sister's asshole, and I was hitting a breaking point that no amount of silicone could fix.

Oliver snapped his fingers once more, bringing me out of my haze. "Earth to Isobel. My office." He gave me an unreadable look before he spun and left.

His butt did amazing things to the pants he wore.

"Really?" The same coworker as before shook her head at me. "Be a tad more obvious, would you?"

"You're right; this weather is a bit gloomy. Best to bring an umbrella tomorrow." I flashed her my most charming smile.

She muttered under her breath before once more concentrating on her computer screen and leaving me alone. Such a good little worker bee.

Chapter 2

Izzy

I stepped into Oliver's office and shut the door behind me with a clink. His space had bachelor written all over it, just another testament to his playboy ways. The room was complete with leather chairs and a bar with expensive scotch. My favorite.

I walked to it and poured us both a drink.

"It's nine a.m.," Oliver chastised as he watched my every move.

It made me suddenly uncomfortable. I could practically feel the lecture he was building up to.

I shrugged my shoulder in faux ease and brought him a glass.

He took it without further comment and gestured for me to sit. I threw the scotch back before taking a seat. I should just sip it, savor the flavor and whatnot, but oh well. The mahogany woodsy flavor was reminiscent of the man currently judging me. I gulped the burn away.

Settling into the chair, I attempted to be my most professional self.

"I know what Harry did was awful," Oliver paused as if searching for the right words, "but can you please stop watching that video on our internet? Our IT team keeps informing me every time a lewd image appears. You know how they are after we had that incident with Peter."

Shit, rookie mistake. Never use public Wi-Fi when watching your ex dick-down someone else. "Apologies, boss man. I know you don't want another Pegging Peter incident."

Let's just say I left all cylindrical objects alone on his desk after he was fired. His sparkly stapler was on mine now though—right on top of my pile of manhwas—it was one of my favorite possessions. I may have a bit of an obsession with anything bright and colorful.

Oliver's brow wrinkled and his full lips flattened into a line. He sighed, exasperated. "Look. You have two more weeks of this moping bullshit. Then you need to cut it out. You didn't even love the man."

"Oh, so it's tough-love-bestie Oliver then?" I straightened in my seat and gave him my most cantankerous expression.

His face finally relaxed into a smile. He brought his scotch up, sipping it slowly. How incredibly proper of him."We both know I'm only the figurehead, not the actual boss here. Why you choose to work amongst the lot still confuses me."

He wasn't wrong. This company was technically mine, but I didn't especially like it. When I started, we were a marketing platform to promote the underdog. Now it felt like all we did was help schedule posts and keep up with trends on social media. I enjoyed the back side of it: finding patterns, tracking algorithms, projecting shifts. Unfortunately, I didn't particularly have the model beauty that sold—tall, skinny, and all sharp angles—so early on I asked Oliver to be the face of the company.

"Why do I feel hated by my coworker..." I wracked my head for the woman's name that sat next to me. "Sue," I decided on.

Oliver's shit-eating grin somehow expanded. "Well for starters, her name is Kathy."

I shrugged; he couldn't convince me those were different names. Sues and Kathys were the same. If you know, you know.

"And secondly, you really don't know the rumors?" He was holding in his laughter at this point.

"Rumors?" I questioned.

"You're fucking the boss to keep your job." He was full belly laughing now.

"Ha. Ha. Ha," I replied humorlessly. So maybe occasionally I would get drunk and leave when I felt like it. What's wrong with working from home?

Oliver sobered. "Are you sure you're going to be okay? We have our reunion coming up."

I growled out loud, "Oh, exactly what I need. Why are we going to that again?"

Oliver placed an elegant finger to his beautiful lips. "Marketing perhaps?"

"You've got jokes." At this point, I might rather wear beads out of a New Orleans puddle on Bourbon Street during Mardi Gras than go to this reunion.

"Room is already booked, luxury suite and all. Adjoining rooms. A spa. It'll be a vacation." Oliver was clearly enjoying my misery.

Hah. Our high school was exactly the last place I aspired to go. I was the overweight scholarship girl that wore hand-me-downs, but Oliver had a point. This would be an excellent marketing opportunity. Half of our old classmates were D-class celebrities that could switch to our company for all their self-promotion needs. More importantly, I could flaunt as the confident epicurean businesswoman I became.

Another unfortunate annoyance was my step-sister; she would undoubtedly be at the reunion. I wondered if she would bring precious Harry as her date. No, thank you.

When my father passed unexpectedly, my mother immediately upended our lives and moved us across the country. During that period, our relationship deteriorated, and we grew incredibly distant. We hadn't fully unpacked into our new home, when my mother met my step-sister's dear old dad at a school event. After they married, I only spoke to my mother at our sporadic family dinners, and even that felt unbearable.

My father. Fuck, I missed him. I was the queen of pushing my feelings deep into the recesses of my mind and I still hadn't processed his death even after all these years. It might have something to do with the lack of closure. My mother didn't bother to plan a funeral for him before we were hightailing it across state lines and changing our last names to further "distance" us from the pain.

I rolled my head between my shoulders to release some of my anxiety and relinquish the memories of him.

I would go to therapy. One day.

The last reason I so desperately didn't want to go to the reunion? Well, that was a secret I planned on keeping. And another point towards me needing professional help.

At least I would have Oliver and my other friend, Yara.

"Is Yara staying with us?" I lifted myself off the chair, peeling my thighs up as I went and deemed it was a two glasses of scotch kind of day. I poured another finger, threw it back, and resettled in his uncomfortable chair. Leather did not make a sweaty girl comfy.

Oliver once more followed my every move with his eyes. I could practically taste his judgment and I stuck my tongue out at him.

"Floor below, so you won't have to hear the gremlin." He snorted. "That is if she doesn't end up passing out drunk with you. *Again*." He narrowed his eyes in annoyance. Yara and Oliver never did solidify a good friendship; they were amicable and liked to fuck with each other like siblings. I knew that was for my sake, I was the common ground that kept them in each other's orbits.

I had two friends from high school. Well, there was a third, but we weren't exactly friends. I shook my head clearing my thoughts of the man,

I hadn't heard from him since the summer after I graduated. He was just another secret I had kept from Oliver and Yara. They were the only two that really counted. Oliver and I ended up owning this company together. But Yara? She had a completely different career path.

She basically ran a dating service, but for those with *special* interests. Specifically bordering on the *taboo.* It was something I always found intriguing, but I'd never had the courage to pursue the ventures she provided. I almost did once, but then Harry dug his way into my life.

He and I met at a party, and while I wasn't immediately drawn to him, he love-bombed me until I gave in to a date. He kept at it until I agreed to be his. It was at that point Harry completely shifted to shine through as the asshole he truly was. I should have noticed the red flags, but I was desperate to meet a good man, so I ignored them. Once again. He kept me from Yara's dating site before, but nothing would stop me this time around.

The last time Yara and I booked adjacent rooms, she brought her work home with her. Needless to say, the noises kept me from getting much sleep. And I would never admit it out loud but listening to the *activities* had made me horny as hell.

I swept my hair back, removing it from the hole it had fallen into AKA my cleavage. For a moment, I thought I saw something akin to lust sweep through Oliver's eyes, but I dismissed it. He had always drawn a very firm line between us.

Business and pleasure never ended well anyway. Just ask Pegging Peter.

"You have two weeks to accept that we're going." Oliver raised a challenging brow.

"Okay *dad.* Now can I go back to work, boss man?"

Oliver's deep chuckle followed me as I exited his office. I determined it might be best to not actually do any work in this condition. A video call to my bestie was in fact the primo decision.

She answered on the third ring as I exited the building and made my way to my car. My driver/friend, Maddox, somehow always knew when I was enroute and he held the back door open for me.

I let my eyes meet his guarded smoky gray ones for just a moment, before I redirected my attention to my phone. He was another man that was definitively off limits.

Yara's golden hair and beautiful face filled my phone's screen as I settled into the backseat. Her striking cerulean eyes always held a glint of her inner deviance.

"Yara, I'm ready. For real this time. Help a girl out."

"I thought you'd never ask!" Yara's angelic face immediately darkened, turning her into a predator.

I shivered involuntarily at her reaction.

"Fucking finally!! No take backsies." Her high-pitched animated voice was at odds with her calculating eyes. "No more falling on these trash men. It's time." Her excitement was palpable through the phone. It was contagious.

Yara was right. It had been too long; the internet and shitty porn weren't enough. I wanted to fulfill myself. I wanted to delve into my fantasies.

Harry had never given me close to anything I needed, and the one time I tried to communicate with him? He shut down and shamed me. I didn't dare bring it up again.

I thought he only liked missionary, but apparently, I could have gotten a dry dick in my ass, too. God, he fucking sucked. What was I even thinking dating him?

If a man was a walking red flag AND he couldn't make you come? Leave his ass.

I needed to go outside my comfort zone and try something that even just the thought of, had me clenching my thighs together needily. I rubbed my legs against each other, trying to relieve some of the tension that was building up. I had an idea for how this evening was going to play out.

Yara set her phone down, balancing it, and steepled her hands together jokingly. "You're going to go home and rub one out, aren't you?" she cackled loudly. "Good, prep yourself. I am about to help facilitate the ruination of your sex life. You will never be able to go back to these useless men again."

Fuck, she knew me too well. I flicked her off before ending the call.

I had felt the weight of Maddox's eyes during the entire interaction, and I finally met his gaze through the mirror. "You heard none of that!" I poked him in the back of his broad muscular shoulder.

The man was a sexy giant, but unfortunately, he made his intentions clear when it came to me.

Friends only.

I still remembered the night we met, when he kissed me in a bar all those years ago. It was soul crushingly hot, and the thought had me burning. I needed to get out of this car. *Now.*

"Izzy..." His voice held its typical warning tone. He was supposed to solely be my driver, not a bodyguard or my dad, but he obviously didn't understand the job assignment.

One lecture from Oliver was enough. Before Maddox could make it two, we pulled up to my house, and I hopped out of the car. I offered him a mocking salute before quickly making my way inside.

Chapter 3

Oliver

His Isobel

Oliver unclenched his hands from his pants as Isobel shut the door behind her when she left. He already texted Maddox to let him know her condition and that she would be on the way after she drank that second glass of alcohol.

It was almost time. He would have his Isobel soon. He had watched over her for years and kept his distance for her own sake. But now? After another easy-to-sway man, Oliver recognized it was doing more damage than good. He would open her eyes to what she really needed. To be his.

Because that's what Isobel was and always had been. *His*.

He had allowed her to explore and find herself, but he had run out of patience. He tugged out his phone and glanced at the notification; she was calling Yara.

He didn't like that, Isobel should only talk to *him* about her problems, but anything to keep her happy. He supposed.

He still remembered when he first met her.

She was new to his town. She was gloriously beautiful in a way he wasn't used to.

She was also standing on his father's grave. Again.

What the fuck?

"What are you doing?" After a week of watching her, he finally had enough of her disrespect. He walked out of the woods and approached the woman. From a distance, he thought she was older than him, her tempting curves pushing out her clothing in an intoxicating way, but upon his approach, he stiffened.

She turned fully towards him and their close proximity allowed him to observe the roundness of her cheeks, the innocence in her eyes, the tears that rolled down her face.

She was young. Too young. Why was she in this cemetery all alone for the fifth time this week? It wasn't safe. There were bad men in this town.

What the fuck?

She wiped her face with the back of her hand and hardened her shoulders. "What do you want, can't you see I'm mourning?" Her voice came out soft and sweet, even with her evident annoyance.

Oliver felt uncomfortable; was he lusting over not only an underage girl, but a long lost relative he didn't know about?

"You knew my dad?" He finally met her eyes and his breath caught.

They were iridescent, the shade brightened by the sheen from her tears.

"What? No. You idiot. I'm mourning my *dad. James."*

James? That wasn't his dad's name. Okay, so she was insane. That made more sense.

The strange girl tucked a piece of her long silky hair behind her ear. His eyes focused on her ear. It was cute, freckled, and poking out just a bit.

"Mine isn't buried here; he's buried somewhere in California. Or so my mother *says." She appraised him guardedly. "Wait, your dad? Our dads*

died on the same day. Well, yours died two years prior, but the date was the same."

The statement caught Oliver off-guard, and ice slipped into his veins. Nobody talked to him about his dad's death. The suicide had made public news, but nobody spoke a word to him about it.

Instead, his 'friends' just wanted to party and drink and fuck. They were plastic and fake and boring.

He wasn't interested in any of that, but he was doing what he thought the world preferred. Golden boys stayed out of trouble. They could easily hide in the shadows. They could get away with more.

The girl fell down onto the ground dramatically on top of where his father was buried. "Sit with me?"

Her complete disregard of his presence had him smiling genuinely for the first time in years. He gently placed himself next to her, accepting that she had zero etiquette when it came to gravesites.

"I never got to mourn my dad. I get the feeling you didn't either." Her voice was laced in understanding.

He couldn't keep the shock off his face as he turned to look at her again.

She grinned up at him; even sitting, she was much smaller than him. She reminded him of his collection of butterflies. Fragile, beautiful, bright. Except she still had her wings.

He could fix that.

"I can see it in your eyes, the hurt and mistrust. You need to let it out. That's what my dad used to say."

He was curious what else she could glimpse in him. Could she perceive the darkness that threatened to take hold? The anger he held deep in his heart? The need to be in control?

Before he knew what she was doing, she leaned forward abruptly and started hitting his father's gravestone. Beating it over and over again as she screamed profanities. He jerked out of his paralysis and took her hands in his. They were soft, small, and bloodied.

"Stop it," he murmured softly. He didn't think, he simply acted. He softly tugged the girl into his lap and held onto her. Comforting her. He had never been this intimately close to another person. Her face fell into the crook of his neck. He leaned down, breathing her in. Sweet. Floral. Delicious.

Oliver knew he wasn't normal, and he hid that from the world, but he wondered if she could be different. If she was just crazy enough to understand him. To not run away. He felt her shake as she began to sob into his shoulder.

"I miss him so much. And nobody is here to talk to. No one has even told me they're sorry he died. My mother simply shoved it under 50mg antidepressants and a new husband."

He felt an incredibly foreign feeling bubble into his gut. One that took him several moments to truly process.

He was protective over the stranger. He inexplicably cared about her feelings. He undeniably wanted to know more about her.

He had always felt closed off from the world as if a thin filament stood between him and any living being. But sitting here? With this girl in his lap? He could really feel her. He didn't sense that separation.

He didn't believe in love at first sight. But obsession? That was something he was intimately familiar with.

After that encounter, Oliver found himself hyper-fixating on her. He would continue to "accidentally" run into her. He found out she was a freshman and transferred to her school as a senior. He kept everyone else away from her. Except the gremlin named Yara.

He and his Isobel became incredibly close until one day it got to a point where he almost crossed the line. It was a jarring encounter, and it became clear he needed to leave. She was too pure for him. She deserved better, and he would break her.

He enlisted in the military and did his best not to look back; it was the most difficult and selfless decision he ever made. He forced himself to believe he wouldn't return. It was a lie.

When he visited home during his last year of service, Isobel found him and begged him to help her get out of their town. He could tell something bad had happened, but no matter how much he tried to find out, she never told him.

It still drove him crazy to think about it. His mind swirling at the what ifs.

He recalculated his choice. He would never be letting her go. He would always watch over her and keep her safe. And one day when she was ready?

She would be his.

His throbbing cock brought him back to the present.

Without further delay, he wrenched open his pants and pulled out his dick. It was immediately hard the moment she was even within his sight. The instant he thought of her.

Every part of her was a temptation. The freckles that covered only her ears and nowhere else. Her voice that always came out a soothing lilt, even in her rage. Her silky soft skin that he wished to stroke for hours as he watched her come undone.

Her stupidly sweet soul that attracted the worst kinds of monsters. Her insanity that threatened even his own. Her fiery passion for anything she decided she wanted.

It was all of that and more that saved her from him all those years ago. What made him decide to let her keep her wings. Why he wanted to give her a choice, let her choose when she was ready for every twisted part of his soul. He had never been obsessed with a girl before her. It had always been items, things, those who did him wrong.

She installed those cameras to catch Harry. She had asked for Oliver's help. He was more than happy to set them up for her. Happier still when she didn't remove them. They made her feel safe.

Oliver watched her on them every evening as she went to sleep. That was if he couldn't make it to her house. Which he did most nights. He had a key, so he was basically invited inside. She just didn't know about his nightly visits. *Yet.*

Oliver discerned she was slowly gaining a romantic interest in him. Over the years he went from her protector to her best friend and now it was time for the next step.

He called Maddox as he fisted his cock, checking to ensure his door was still fully shut. "News?"

"Target has arrived home. Friend might be a problem. Touched base with Milo for an update on the other situation."

Oliver cursed under his breath as he stroked his length up and down. Her smell still saturated his office. Honeysuckles. That's the closest way he could describe it. It intoxicated him more than any drink could, and he desperately wanted a taste.

He didn't disconnect the call as he opened his computer screen, flipped to her camera feed, and watched her undress. He continued his frantic stroke up and down his dick. The tension began to coil tightly.

"Two weeks until our trip. It's time."

Maddox grunted. "You sure she's ready?"

Oliver's face twisted into a dark shape reminiscent of a grin. He watched on his monitor as Isobel began her own ministrations. He yanked his dick hard as she lathered lube and pushed her double-sided dildo deep into her body.

"Yes," he confirmed, ending the call.

He continued to watch through the screen as she rubbed furious circles on her clit while she pushed her toy in and out of her pliable body. The toy she thought she had drunkenly bought. The one he had actually purchased for her. Did her subconscious know to prepare her for what was to come? Oliver's grip on his dick tightened, until it was just on the edge of pain, as he continued his furious strokes. Her build up was clear even through the screen and her pumps increased as his did.

He lifted off of the seat, pushing into his hand, and came with a grunt as her mouth opened in ecstasy.

His patience had just run out.

Even if she wasn't, he would make her ready.

Chapter 4
Izzy

I spent the next two weeks pointedly ignoring the world. I wasn't exactly hurt by Harry, but man was it embarrassing. Especially the family dinner I was supposed to attend. Hard pass on that. And he still denied it? How could he lie when I literally caught him on camera? Men.

After I captured the video of his infidelity, I made him meet me in a neutral location—a café—and I showed him the evidence. He had the audacity to say I made it with AI. That it was my fault he was with my step-sister now, that I pushed him to her when I spewed my accusations. Needless to say, that was the end of just another pointless relationship with a horribly immature, vanilla man.

My step-sister and I had never been close, but now I did my best to prevent any possible interactions.

I was a bit annoyed, though. Usually, I would be venting all of this to Oliver, but it almost felt as if he was avoiding me. What gave?

I voiced these exact concerns to Yara on the phone as I opened my bag to pack for our trip.

"He's probably just giving you space. You know, girl time and what have you." That did sound almost convincing.

"I guess..." I still didn't fully believe it. Oliver always stayed by my side for every fucked man and break up over the years. It was odd he was keeping his distance now, but I chalked it up to our impending trip.

She paused, almost as if she was unsure if she should continue, it was very uncharacteristic of Yara. "And truthfully? Isn't Oliver a little bit *too* involved in your life? He even freaking tracks your phone!"

I didn't want to rehash this argument. She always said there was something off with how close Oliver and I were. In all honesty, I think she might have simply been jealous that he and I spent so much time together while she lived on the other side of the country.

Humming, I walked into my bathroom gathering what I would need for my trip. I opted to change the topic entirely. "Are you there yet?"

Our high school resided in good ol' sunny Florida. While Oliver graduated three years my senior, I would be bringing him as my plus one to our ten-year reunion. I was still dreading it, but I could acknowledge the potential for expanding our company.

Our profit was just teetering on the cusp of me never needing to work another day again, and I could one hundred percent support that. I preferred to delegate, if at all possible.

"Not yet," Yara stated casually, accepting the shift and my obvious disagreement with her opinions on Oliver.

"I am excited about one thing though." I redirected the conversation again as I organized my toiletries bag. "Sooo, you find someone for me?"

Yara cackled in my ear, "Girl, you know how this works, but yes of course. I will have it all ready to go the night of the reunion. You sure you want to go in completely blind?"

I set my toiletries bag on my bed next to my suitcase. My ever-active libido was more excited than I thought possible and with myself placed firmly in the friendzone for both Oliver and Maddox, I needed options. "Yes, I have a special request in mind for our first encounter, and I don't really care what he looks like. Just make sure he knows what he's getting himself into. I don't want to be rejected, *please*?" I whined the last word as

I pinched a stomach roll through my shirt. I didn't overeat and I worked out, but even still, I never could make much of a difference to my size.

"Girl, when are you going to wake up and realize those thick thighs, big old TDs, and juicy ass are what men dream of?"

I scoffed. "Harry certainly didn't agree." I was still in the whiny and pity party phase of our breakup. My step-sister was gorgeous in all the ways I, most certainly, was not.

Yara made a series of noises that reminded me of an exhaust backfiring, and I pulled the phone from my ear, hissing.

"Ouch," I grunted.

"Shut your whore mouth, you know that man is trash. He didn't deserve you, let alone this self-deprecating bullshit. I know the man for you, I found him a year ago and he wanted you then. All the same, he wants you now. We both just waited ever so patiently for your call. And he's hot AF."

"Sure," I replied in disbelief and continued packing my bag. My hands hovered over my underwear drawer.

Fuck it. Was the man even worth it if he didn't want you in a Mumu?

"I can hear your brain through the phone."

"Do I need to pack lingerie?" I questioned. I wasn't exactly sure how this worked.

"Girl. Why bother? Easy access is what I always say. And all those strings and shit? Well, if it makes you feel good, but if not–" she paused "–wear what makes you feel the best."

Decision made, I dropped the lingerie that rode right up my ass back into the drawer. "Mumu it is."

Yara laughed. "You know I love you, right?"

"Always," I confirmed. "So, you going to tell me about your newest beau?"

Yara went unexpectedly silent. "I don't have one," she finally stated.

It was odd, as she was always dishing the tea on the newest flame in her life, but I knew when Yara didn't want to talk about something. We may live states away, but we always got each other.

"Seriously though, can we talk about Maddox? Why don't you just jump on *that*? He watches you even more closely than Oliver does," Yara not so subtly redirected.

I choked and dropped what I was holding to the floor. "Funny. You've got jokes."

When I first met Maddox, I thought he might be interested, but he had fully friendzoned me. I realized I wasn't his type; he seemed to be into the gym babes while I was an anime, bookish, nerd girl.

"Sure..." Yara drawled the word out. "Well finish your packing. T-minus twelve hours until we are finally reunited. It has been too long. In case you were wondering," she scolded me.

"Yeah, yeah, I know. In our next lives we can both strive to not be the boss ass bitches we are and actually have more time for each other."

She cackled into my ear, "We have way too much energy for that." She turned the phone, and I heard her yell at someone. "Got to go, this boss ass bitch is about to meet your future man. See you soon, doll face."

The phone clicked and I sat it down, moving my attention to my now fully packed bag.

Six Mumus, one pair of socks, and a t-shirt.

Well, that would not work. I dumped my entire bag and restarted the process. I had a plane to catch and a man to fuck. I scanned the time on my phone and cursed.

Why did I always procrastinate everything?

Chapter 5

Izzy

I was drunk. I grasped Oliver's hand on my right and Maddox's hand on my left. Flying was cool and all but frankly? I was overstimulated. The height, the buzz of noise around us, the barely working AC, the recycled air. None of it was good for my anxiety and it caused me to drink. Heavily. It was a testament to my current intoxicated state.

I let go of Oliver's hand to turn my music up. Again. I was definitely hammered at this point, but I didn't especially want them to know. My overprotective men.

More importantly, why did I not splurge for better seats? Why had I agreed to this stupid reunion? And why was I wedged between two burly men?

Anytime I moved, their arms brushed against mine. My skin tingled at the contact, and I tried to jerk away from one, only to push into the other. I couldn't win.

I swiveled my head shooting them both aggressive glares and they laughed at me. *Rude*.

I narrowed my eyes in an over dramatic way, I could still hear their laughter, even through my headphones.

As if on cue, my bladder decided that it was time for me to make my exit from these annoying men. I began detangling myself from them, before heading to the plane bathroom.

Why anyone would fuck in a plane bathroom made no sense to me. They were tiny and smelled like chemicals. And why were there so many seats shoved together? And why was my skin so sweltering hot and these rows so tiny to wedge my ass through? Someone was going to turn and -BAM- face full of sweaty ass. Gross.

Intrusive thoughts continued to infiltrate my muddled mind as I did my business. Five shots deep and I was most certainly drink. Drunk?

I didn't want to outwardly portray it, but in reality, I bit off more than I could chew. I'd told Yara I was ready; I was no longer so sure. Plus, the height wasn't helping. Being up high had frayed my nerves ever since my senior year of high school.

I shut that line of thought down and added it to the list I would talk to my future therapist about.

Stepping out of the airplane bathroom, I stumbled right into a wall.

"Wall, move please." The words slurred a bit as they left my lips.

The Wall moved, what a good receptive Wall.

It steadied me, and with blurry eyes, I tried to focus on it. "Bella, are you alright?" the Wall spoke, the voice was a deep baritone that sent an unwanted shiver down my spine.

I tried to steady my gaze on the Wall, but my face was pressed directly into it.

I felt pressure on my shoulders as Maddox stepped in behind me to pull me from the Wall. Maddox's firm grasp was unmistakable as he dragged me away, and I never got the chance to even properly see my Wall.

"Always catching attention. I swear," Maddox grumbled as he placed me back firmly into my seat. He reached across, buckling me in before resettling next to me.

Drunk Izzy enjoyed the manhandling. It wasn't entirely fair. I spent most of my time enveloped in these two rousing men, unwanted by either.

Where Oliver gave a very clear boy-next-door vibe, Maddox was the older rugged protector type that you craved to witness go full teddy bear mode. Maddox's size was impressive and even when we were sitting it was difficult to meet his sharp gray eyes. Instead, I used my proximity to refamiliarize myself with his ink that spilled out across corded muscles and encompassed the entirety of both his arms.

Without meaning to, I absentmindedly traced one of the tattooed lines on his bicep closest to mine.

Maddox stiffened and Oliver, noticing the movement, reached over and yanked my hand off of him.

"I think you have reached your limit." Oliver's voice was calm, but I saw a fire flash through his typically cool eyes.

"Never any fun. I'm telling Yara on you." I scrunched my nose in annoyance.

Oliver frowned at me before reaching up to rub his temples and muttering under his breath.

"Maddox, tell boss man he's being too strict and controlling. He never lets me do *anything,*" I grumbled, crossing my arms over my chest dramatically.

Oliver followed the movement and his lips flattened into a line. He almost looked constipated.

I turned to Maddox, his eyes crinkled in amusement, but even in my state, I could tell he was on edge. "Baby girl, you know he's right. You over drank."

Fuck, if Maddox was agreeing I knew I was in trouble.

"Fineeeeeee." The word came out dramatically long. Oliver was a control freak, but I secretly loved that about him. Being told what to do by a sexy man? Yes, please.

Maddox, well, he didn't speak too much. In fact, sometimes it seemed like Oliver and I were the only ones he graced his words with at all. Which meant when he said something, I listened, within reason.

Oliver poked my cheek. "I still can only guess what goes through that mind of yours."

I turned my head to him, squinting my eyes and furrowing my eyebrows dramatically. "You'll never know."

But did he say nap? I felt my eyelids suddenly gain weight, and my body relaxed fully into the seat. Uncrossing my arms, I reached down and yanked up my handy dandy blanket. Pulling the arm rest up, I snuggled into Oliver's side. I forced him to be my pillow and allowed myself to succumb to my alcohol induced coma.

My flying skills were *top notch*.

Chapter 6

Oliver

His Isobel

Oliver used every ounce of self-control he had not to rip down Isobel's leggings and fuck her here and now on the plane.

She moaned softly in her sleep, snuggling closer to his side.

His grip on his pants tightened.

He focused his attention on Maddox. "Why does she never listen to me? She always looks to you. It's frustrating."

Maddox chuckled softly. "Because you're an overbearing control freak that tracks her every second of the day and her subconscious is telling her what her brain doesn't. You're dangerous." Maddox's eyes turned soft as Isobel shifted again.

Oliver glanced down to make sure she was fast asleep before responding. "That's rich coming from you. You were the one that came up with the idea to get Harry away from her."

Maddox grunted, "It was too easy. I barely did anything at all. I got Milo to send him a text from Hallie's number, the rest was on him."

Isobel moved again letting out a raspy sigh.

Oliver stiffened. Everywhere. "This trip. We can't wait any longer. It's time."

"Agreed. You good?" Maddox nodded his head at Isobel.

"No," Oliver admitted.

"I didn't think so. Here I'll help."

Maddox lifted the arm rest between himself and Isobel and took her sleeping form; Oliver allowed it. Oliver may be a control freak, but Maddox's self-control far outweighed Oliver's. They both knew it.

Once she was resituated, Maddox lowered his voice and leaned towards Oliver. "There's a man that has been watching her, five seats back. He ran into her when she exited the restroom. There was something *off*."

She was always running into despicable men. Oliver had done his best over the years to rid her of them, but it was time he staked his claim. He surveyed the area discreetly and found the man Maddox was indicating.

"I am not exactly sure why, but he seems oddly familiar. I'll reach out to Milo about it." Oliver thought aloud.

Oliver spent the rest of the flight discreetly watching the man, ignoring the stiffness in his pants, and trying not to outwardly show his obsession with the sleeping woman.

He was once more grateful for Maddox's presence. Maddox kept Oliver from crossing a line with Isobel.

He just hoped she would be able to accept them both. Together.

Chapter 7
The Wall
His Bella Isa

The Wall was on his third flight in less than forty-eight hours, but also the most important. He had flown from his home, to California, back to his home, and now he was enroute to Florida.

When Yara finally called him, he could barely believe it. The Wall spent the last several years hoping beyond all hope that his Bella Isa would finally come to her senses. That she would return to him. That she would finally realize it was time to let go and fall into her deepest desires. He was afraid she would never take the leap, and he would be forced to go off script and do something drastic. But just before he took matters into his own hands, *it happened.*

When just over a year ago Isa finally joined Yara's 'dating app', the Wall jumped on the chance and joined himself. He used a fake name, and due to numerous physical changes, his pictures were unrecognizable. Yara didn't even figure out who exactly he was.

When that ended up being a false hope and his dear Isa fell into another useless relationship, the Wall began to calculate his next move. When her most recent man fucked up just as all the others had, he decided it was time. One way or another, she would be his. The Wall wouldn't let her get away as she had all those years ago, but he would also *never* take her choice away.

Finally, his patience won out, and he got the call.

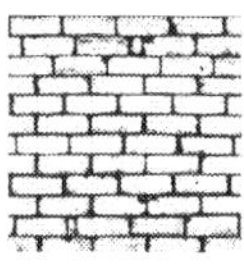

The call came around two weeks prior. He had Yara's number saved, and it didn't even ring once before he was hitting accept.

"Are you still interested in her?" Yara was a no-nonsense kind of person, and he could appreciate that.

"I am. I have not found anyone else that has piqued my fancy yet."

Yara grumbled through the phone, "You can't hurt her. And you will have to meet me in person first for an interview."

"I wouldn't dream of it, and of course I would be more than happy to."

"We won't be reimbursing you for your expenses, and you will be meeting her in a mutual location."

The Wall did his best to not appear too *enthusiastic. He knew on paper he seemed like an upstanding citizen, and he needed Yara to believe that as well. "Of course, send me the details and I will be there."*

Less than twenty-four hours ago he "met" Yara in person and, as he suspected, she still didn't recognize him. Now here he was, watching his Bella Isa from only feet away. She was still crowded by those two men: Oliver and Maddox. The obsession they both had to her was clear as day, and the Wall contained his scalding rage as Maddox shifted her into his side.

Neither were good enough for her and they would both be problematic, but that was a matter for another day.

First things first, he had a reunion to attend.

Chapter 8

Izzy

We made it to the hotel, and I was officially lying across a large luxuriously comfortable bed in my outfit from the plane. I didn't exactly remember how I got here, but I imagined Maddox or Oliver carried me.

At this point in our friendships, I wasn't even embarrassed, just surprised either could handle my weight and were able to get me up here.

I fluttered my eyes a few times before meeting Oliver's worried gaze.

"Maybe a bit less next flight?" His attitude did nothing to help the pounding that threatened to break apart my skull.

"Yes, boss man. You know how heights are for me though."

His features softened. "I know," he finally expelled.

He long since knew not to question me on why; when he visited home from his military tour, I suddenly hated heights. The last time he tried to push me on it, I wouldn't talk to him for a week.

He moved to the side of the cushioned bed and leaned fully over me, his hair tickling my face as he appeared to have an internal battle. He finally settled on, "I'm worried. About you and about you going to the reunion."

His lips were inches from my face and my gaze caught on their shape. Focused on what they would feel like. On how he would taste.

I jerked further back into the bed and grunted at him. I was so horny that even horribly hungover, my ever-active sex drive was holding the reins.

He stood back up to his full height, towering over me with an emotionless mask shrouding his features. There was another reason he was the face of our company past his good looks, he was a master at hiding any and all of his inner thoughts.

That was most definitely not a skill set I excelled in. Which is why he would be the one in charge of mingling at the reunion. Which, again, had me questioning why I even needed to go.

The reunion.

There were two distinguishable men that might be there.

One that I would run from and one that I wanted to run to.

Oliver knew this reunion wasn't on my top priorities list. What I had kept, even from his protective self, was that there was a bit more to why I didn't want to return. And I was trying my best to not let it slip, because he would lose his ever-loving shit.

Oliver treated me as a damsel in distress at the best of times and the worst of times. I swear he thought I was made of thread. One hard tug and I would be frayed for life.

I attempted my most grumpy face. Eyebrows screwed up, lips pursed, air blown into my cheeks.

Oliver laughed at me. "Are you practicing as an anime cat girl?"

I growled and launched a pillow under me at him.

He dodged it easily.

"That was my mad face, you jerk!"

Oliver nodded his head comically slowly. "Sure, sure. Well, as you know, the reunion is tomorrow night, so ready yourself for that. But first, she-who-must-not-be-named has arrived. She has been screaming at me for hours to let her in here to torment you."

"Yara?" I sat up excitedly forgetting my hangover. While we talked almost daily, I hadn't been face-to-face with Yara in months. "Why didn't you lead with that, you big oaf?" I launched another pillow at said oaf a bit more aggressively than the last.

The movement lifted my blouse up over my belly while simultaneously jiggling my titties more than should be possible.

Instead of dodging this time, his eyes caught on the movement and I suddenly became self-conscious.

The pillow hit him in the stomach with a *thunk* before dropping to the ground.

"I know, I need to get to the gym with you and Maddox."

His gaze darkened, and a face I had never seen before adorned his features. His hands tightened to fists. A shiver crept up my spine and I almost felt scared. Of Oliver? I blinked my eyes and whatever I thought I saw, was gone.

"I told you; you are perfect exactly the way you are, Isobel." Oliver's voice held no room for argument, his eyes holding mine in a trance. They were fathomless dark abysses that seemed to want to convey more to me than I could understand.

"Oh no, not my birth name. Dad is MAD," I joked uncomfortably, trying to get away from whatever this was.

It had the wanted effect and Oliver flashed his teeth in a grin. "I'll let the gremlin in."

He offered me one more indecipherable intense look before turning and heading to the door.

Chapter 9

Izzy

"Can you believe it? This man basically waited for you. He is interested in everything you want and has exactly the same boundaries." Yara and I were now lying on my bed in our comfiest clothes. She wore a t-shirt and sweats. And I wore my notorious Mumu. This one was bright fluorescent pink and incredibly soft. So comfortable. I needed all I could get with the hangover still threatening to take hold.

Drinking just gets more and more painful with age, and at twenty-eight, I was lucky if I only needed one day of recovery.

I refocused on our conversation and paused the trash TV we were watching. Something about how if you're in love, you never lie to your partner. The premise itself was a joke. "Honestly it sounds great but like, almost too great. Isn't that a red flag?"

Yara laughed and rolled until she lay on her side, facing me. "I know what you mean, and a girl can never be too careful, but Izzy, he checked out. Background check, references, the whole shebang. I also cross-checked the name with anyone that you might have run into or know, and he came back clean."

I still had an uncomfortable feeling deep in my gut that I knew better than to ignore. "And, you're sure? You met him too, right?"

Yara's face sobered as she realized the extent of my anxiety, she lifted a hand up and hauled me to her in a hug. Yara was more a sister than my step-sister had ever been, and I allowed myself to soak in the comfort she provided. It calmed some of my worries, but I couldn't ignore that there was something deep in the recesses of my consciousness that was screaming something wasn't right. But it could just be my return here. And the man I had done my best to forget about.

"I promise, I did every check known to mankind and I made sure he had nothing but green flags. He seems to be an average *sexy* Joe, but with a plethora of desires he is looking to fulfill."

I pushed aside my worries and allowed myself to genuinely believe she might be right. "But he waited for me, why? Isn't that weird? I first tried this over a YEAR ago. No man waits that long for any woman. Especially one he hasn't met. Especially me."

Yara let go to punch me lightly on my shoulder. "Correct! *Especially* you. I'm sure the man has gotten his dick wet but from my conversations with him, he seems to have been stuck on you. Because, again, you are gorgeous! Stop with that self-deprecating bullshit."

I swallowed thickly. "I just got cheated on, I'm sorry my self-confidence isn't at its highest."

Yara's expression turned sympathetic. Her golden locks were spread across the bed and if it weren't for knowing her so well, I would almost think her an angel. She didn't understand what it felt like to not be the standard image of beauty. I was more of an acquired taste, I knew I was beautiful, but I felt I had to convince the world. Every. Single. Day.

While I had not been in love with Harry, I felt trapped in the relationship, and it still hurt when he betrayed me as he did. My mother didn't help in the matter, she suggested I get on a diet and show him what he was missing out on. That my step-sister had done me a *favor*.

The thing about cheaters, though? I could have been the sexiest woman in the world, and he still would have cheated. They always had an excuse ready to go. My brain knew this, but my heart still felt a bit bruised. As did my ego.

"Also, I don't want you to be caught off guard, but I checked on the site last night to see who all RSVP'd to the reunion." I knew where this was going. "And Hallie is coming." Yara paused, watching my expressions closely. "She's bringing a plus one."

Ching, ching, ching. I guessed right. No doubt my step-sister would be bringing Harry as her plus one. "Hallie sure does love to rub anything in my face that she can."

Yara crinkled her nose. "Hallie certainly hasn't changed since high school."

A knock sounded at the hotel door.

"Buuuuuut onto better and brighter things. I took the liberty of ordering us food while you showered."

"You remember..." I began.

"That you're allergic to shellfish. Yes, I let them know. I did get myself shrimp, but I made sure to request separate orders and that they would be liable for your death if they fuck it up."

"Dramatic." I watched Yara as she got up and grabbed her food from the person at the door.

All I saw was a giant form before she shut the door with an odd look on her face.

"You good?" I questioned, sitting up on the bed.

Yara's face shifted. "Yeah, I just thought I recognized him from somewhere, but I must be seeing things." She opened the cover off of the food container, shrimp. "Looks like this is mine, I'll sit over there and eat it." She pointed to a table in the corner as far from me as possible.

I gave her an exasperated look. "You know I'm not deathly allergic, right?"

"Sure, sure." Yara was clearly still preoccupied, but another knock sounding distracted my thoughts. I stood up and went to the door for my food.

The delivery boy was very nondescript and could barely be a day over 20. I signed the receipt, adding a tip before taking the food and thanking him. "Not sure if it was the same one, but I didn't recognize whoever it was."

Yara gave me a reassuring smile from across the room and I repositioned myself back on the bed. Raising the cover on the plate, I found a cheeseburger and fries. "How did you know I needed the greasy food?"

"Easy, you were on a plane today." Her tone softened. "You ever going to tell us why you suddenly became deathly afraid of heights?"

"Nope," I replied, popping the *p* aggressively. I lifted the burger to my lips and felt the greasy wonder immediately lift my spirits.

Yara raised an eyebrow but continued her own munching. "I wish I could find a man that looked at me the way you're making eyes at that burger."

I swallowed my bite. "You going to tell me about your newest beau?"

"Nope." Yara threw back at me, popping the *p* around a shrimp tail.

"Touché."

Yara threw a shrimp tail in my direction. "You better watch yourself! Death by flying tail isn't what you want on your gravestone."

We both died laughing at that.

We spent the rest of our evening snuggled in the bed, drinking wine, and watching trash TV.

Fuck, I missed Yara.

Chapter 10

Izzy

"Yara, get up!" I shook my friend aggressively, but she just grumbled. How was it already mid-afternoon? We were going to be late to this horrid affair.

"Don't feel good," she garbled out.

I sighed dramatically. "It was only one bottle of wine and we split it, you are not abandoning me for this."

Yara shot up suddenly and ran to the bathroom. The retching noises were unmistakable.

"You're not pregnant, are you?" I followed Yara and found her a puddle of misery hugging the toilet. Been there, done that. I held her hair and stroked her back as she shuddered.

"Shut up," she gurgled out weakly.

My concern sky-rocketed, this didn't seem normal. Usually she would puke and rally, but this felt like something else. "You're not actually pregnant, are you?"

Yara's response was to vomit into the toilet.

I was officially worried. "Can I get you anything?"

"No." The word echoed around the porcelain.

"You're not going to make it, are you?"

Another dry heave. The noise had me swallowing down my own nausea. Maybe this was a sign I should just bail on the reunion.

And my plans after.

"I'm not. I can't be around those hellions in this condition. I woke up early this morning like this, but I was hoping it would go away." She managed to get the full sentence out before her dry heaving continued. "You are still going through with it. Both things. I have another room booked for you, under an alias. There is a packet I want you to read and an NDA you need to sign. You need this." More puking.

How could I argue with my friend as she became one with the hotel toilet?

Fuck. I was really going to do this. "Okay." I whispered the word.

"Good. In my bag, the folder labeled *Come to Bed*," Yara yakked out.

I stopped stroking her back, if she wasn't in this condition, I might hit her. "You know, you are going to catch these hands. How did you know what my plans were?"

"You forget, I am your best friend and I know everything. Now leave me to my misery. Nothing to do but wait till this passes. Throw me one of those fifty-dollar bottles of water from the mini bar first though, would you?"

"You've got jokes." I used my hair tie to put her hair back the best I could, so it would not endure the radioactive waste below. The smell of vomit permeated the space and I needed to exit this room. Now.

I grabbed one of the unnecessarily expensive hotel water bottles and rolled it to her. "Feel better. You got your phone in case you need me?"

She pulled back from the toilet long enough to lift her phone and wave it at me. "You mean if you need *me*? If you bail on tonight, just know I will never let you live it down." She made another disgusting noise before plummeting back to her new home below.

I could not handle any more of *that* and shut the door with a slink.

"She okay?"

I jumped, turning around. "How does your massive frame always sneak up on me?"

Maddox leaned against the wall across from me. I had not even heard the giant enter. He pointed his thumb at the opened door across from my bed. "Adjoining rooms, not that hard."

That literally didn't explain anything, but that was Maddox. A man of few words.

"Sure. And she'll be fine, I think." I crossed the room to my suitcase. "You're still coming with us, right?" I tried to keep the anxiety out of my tone. I only had the singular plus one, but Maddox was on the list as Yara's since she didn't have anyone else she wanted to bring.

"Wouldn't miss it." His calculating eyes followed my every move. Maddox's military background and close friendship with Oliver made it so I always felt protected in his presence. Except right now. I felt like prey.

Like I was one of his targets. I couldn't understand why I was suddenly feeling that way.

I was beginning to think I was the problem, I kept feeling on edge for no apparent reason.

"What is it?" I finally asked.

"You haven't supplied your plans this evening."

I gulped and did my best to clear my face of emotion. When I agreed to let him be my driver all those years ago, I didn't realize he would act as if he were my bodyguard, too. That he would be with me any time I wasn't in my home or at work. "I uh, am going to meet an old friend."

"No." Maddox's steel gaze was unnerving as I tried to ignore it and take out my outfit for the evening instead. The sparkling rainbow dress was one of my favorite purchases and I knew I would need any support I could get this evening. Even if it was in clothing form.

"You're not my dad. That is Oliver's job if you haven't forgotten."

At that, Oliver stepped from the door adjoining our rooms. The room he and Maddox were sharing.

"What was that?" He surveyed the area. "And where is the gremlin?"

"She is currently occupied on a porcelain throne and will, unfortunately, not be making it." I stood up, dress in hand. "You both have 15 seconds to leave or catch an eyeful of chunk."

Neither made any indication of leaving. Oh well, I wasn't in the mood to argue. I turned and began to strip.

"Isobel." Oliver's tone was threatening. "What are you doing?"

I slid the Mumu over my head, it left me fully naked, but all they could see was my ass. They had seen more than that over the years. Hell, Maddox had walked in on me rubbing one out before and Oliver and I had gone skinny dipping several times back in high school. And besides that? Neither of them wanted me, it made it easier to be comfortable when I wasn't trying to impress either of the men.

I threw the Mumu over my shoulder in their direction. "Getting dressed." I tugged the sparkly sequined rainbow dress over my tits and then my ass.

Maddox let out a disgruntled noise.

I turned back to the men; their expressions were both stormy and I watched as they exchanged a look. "Not anything you both haven't seen before. Anyway, we ready to do this jazz?" I mustered up as much courage as I could.

They swapped one more unreadable look before they both jerked their heads in a nod.

Chapter 11

Maddox

His Ellie

The bane of Maddox's existence. The reason he still lived and breathed. The most magnificent woman he had ever met. *His* Ellie. Isobel.

Maddox met her after his last bodyguarding position. The one where his objective died. Maddox already knew Oliver from years back when they were enlisted together. Except Oliver ended up leaving immediately after his four years. Oliver told Maddox, at the time, there was something more important for him to go back to. Maddox found out later that it was Isobel.

Maddox didn't blame Oliver. She affected everyone around her, and she didn't even realize it. The most oblivious prey.

But to Maddox? She was his tether to reality. She was what kept him from losing his mind and destroying everything in his path.

That's all Maddox was before he met her. Destruction.

Maddox had a few good years in the private sector after he finally left the service. Until the person he was supposed to protect died. Maddox took a bullet to the shoulder in his attempt to keep them safe. It was pointless. Their location was disclosed by another person in the company for a quick payday. It was then and there that Maddox lost the last of his faith in humanity. Where he finally let the years of suffering catch up to him.

He would never forget as the girl he was supposed to keep safe bled out in his hands. Her choking last breaths. Her cries for her mother. Her eyes as she realized that she wouldn't be making it.

She was *ten* years old, and he had failed her. The world had failed her. No death prior had affected him as hers had.

Maddox wasn't a good man, he had hurt more than he had saved, but he thought the private sector would do some good. That it would finally be a turning point for him.

With the failure of that, he had felt like he was floating with nothing to tie him down and keep him grounded.

He was essentially alone in the world, and he was determined to drink himself into an early grave. He was five days into a bender when she found him.

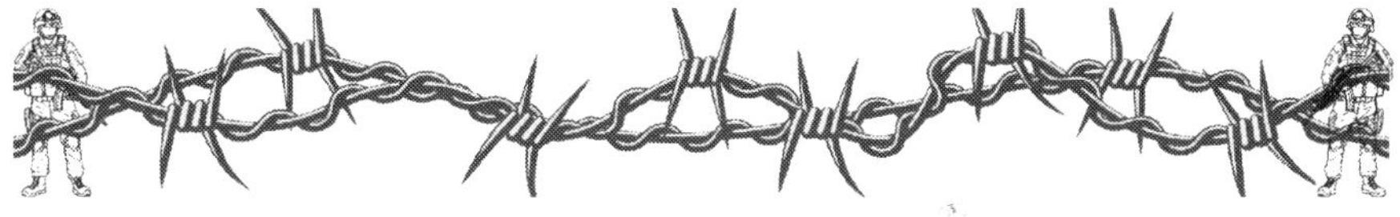

"You come here often?"

The silky voice infiltrated Maddox's stupor, but he didn't move his gaze from the glass in his hand. He assumed it wasn't directed at him.

The same smooth voice laughed softly. "Ouch, it burns. I was just trying to find someone for a good chat. I am officially, once more, disgustingly single. But it's fine, I'll respect your boundaries."

At that, Maddox finally moved to glance towards the noise, and he stiffened. Striking sage green eyes met his, they were a brilliant shade and he found himself lost for a moment before she was snapping her fingers in front of him. He was silently thanking his old military buddy for suggesting this bar.

"You good, my dude?"

He blinked rapidly at that and took in the rest of the beautiful woman attached to the eyes. She was a sexy, curvy, small thing, with a noticeable ferocity. It was in the way she held herself, as if she would fight him if need be. He almost laughed as he thought it.

He didn't believe in love at first sight. But lust? Even in his drunken trance he felt himself harden uncomfortably.

"Earth to strange man at the bar, if you're having a stroke, blink twice."

He met her gaze. "I'm good, sit with me?" He gestured to the vacant chair to his left.

Her brows rose dramatically high, but she sat elegantly beside him. Her curves stretched the shorts she wore delectably, and he forced himself to look away. He adjusted himself as discreetly as possible, before refocusing his eyes on her. It was a mistake. The blouse she wore allowed an unobstructed view of the top of her large chest. His brain was short-circuiting.

"So how about this weather?" the woman quipped softly.

He chuckled humorlessly. "Isn't it storming outside?"

"It is," she confirmed. "So, you want to talk about why you are clearly drowning your sorrows? Or how about a game instead? I am something of a mind reader, I'll have you know."

"Is that right?" He decided to play along with the eclectic girl. He was drawn to her energy. He needed it. Maddox flagged the bartender. "Her drinks on me, and can you grab me a coffee?"

"Rumple shaken," the woman advised the bartender when he turned to her expectantly.

Maddox snorted. "You are over 21, aren't you?"

"I'll have you know I quite like my alcoholic mouthwash. Get drunk while keeping your breath minty fresh, but Scotch is always a good second."

Maddox smiled at her. "So, before we start your mind-reading. How about a name?"

The bartender returned with their drinks, fast as usual. Ellie threw the shot back in one impressive gulp and Maddox averted his eyes from the column of her throat as she swallowed, the way her eyes glassed over, how the movement jostled her chest. She was enthralling. He wanted his hand around her throat, his lips on her neck. The thought startled him. Maddox, instead, chugged down the lukewarm black coffee, ignoring the flavor. He didn't want anything about this woman to be forgotten or to make a fool of himself. He couldn't remember the last time he spoke to a woman as interesting as her. Or to anyone at all for that matter. He needed the jolt to clear his mind.

"Isobel. But most everyone calls me Izzy."

He didn't plan on being "most everyone." "I'm Maddox, can I call you Ellie?" He didn't tell her about it also being his first pet's name. He doubted she would appreciate the namesake.

She let out a lyrical laugh. "Of course, Mad dog."

Maddox grumbled at her, and she placed a soft hand on his, stroking it.

"I kid, I kid. Maddox is fitting."

Maddox tried to ignore her touch, but as she went to pull her hand away, he reached out and grabbed it. "I'm sorry," he stated. Startled at his own actions he dropped her hand. "I haven't been touched in awhile," he divulged sheepishly.

Ellie gave him a soft smile, it wasn't pity in her eyes, but something else. She placed her small, smooth hand back on his. "I understand, sometimes when I'm touch-starved, I make my best friend hold me, just to feel something."

A flash of unwarranted jealousy radiated through Maddox, startling him. Maddox couldn't help but fall into the woman's touch. She was radiating kindness and empathy. He felt cared about more by this basic stranger than anyone else he had known for years.

Most of the world turned their back on damaged men. And Maddox was most assuredly damaged.

"Hm, my mind reading might have to wait. As it's a two-handed sort of thing, but how about twenty questions?"

Maddox raised a brow; the coffee was doing its job and he felt himself become more coherent. He gave her another appraising look, doing his best to ignore her curves. "You are *over 21, aren't you?" He was mostly joking.*

"Hardee har har." She flagged the bartender down and ordered another drink. "I would offer you one, but I think the coffee was a good choice. Join me at the booth?" She pointed behind them, and Maddox found he wanted nothing more than to have her pushed against him in it.

"Yes." He waited until she had her new drink in hand before gently tugging her to the booth. He sat down first. Sliding into the corner, he let her go, so she could make her own seating decision. She set her drink down on the table before joining him. He could barely contain his grunt of appreciation when she pushed into the seat until her body was snug to his.

"This okay, big guy?" She looked up at him through her long lashes.

He didn't think it through, he grabbed her face and pushed his lips to hers. She tasted sweet and floral. Minty. He groaned, deepening the kiss. She allowed him to take all that he could, and he was lost to her soft body. Finally, he gained the self-control to separate himself from her. "That okay?"

He noted her lips were swollen, and he felt incredibly happy at having left his mark.

"I knew there was something burning in that body. You feeling any better?"

He found that he was and nodded slowly.

She gave him a smile. "Well not that I didn't love that, but I don't want to treat you like a rebound when you give main character energy. My last boyfriend? Pretty sure he was an NPC."

Maddox was confused. "NPC?"

"Non-playable character. You know those people that ask you the same three questions every time you see them? Where it almost seems like they're lost to the same daily loop?" she explained in her soft soothing voice.

That actually did make sense, and Maddox grunted in agreement.

"Well, you seem like someone that wouldn't be boring. You would make everyday different and unique."

If by that she was alluding to his growing obsession with her, he couldn't disagree. "Thank you?" he questioned.

"You're welcome. Now first things first. Why were you watching your drink like it was the last thing you were going to do?"

Maddox wasn't sure what it was about her, but the next thing he knew, he began telling her his entire life story. He started with his stint in foster care, continued with his time in the military, and ended with his last job. He spoke more words to her than he probably had in the last year, but he just couldn't stop, and they continued to spill out.

Every time he shared something traumatic or especially awful, she would lean into him more or squeeze his hand. He never felt any shame or pity; all he felt was a warm, comforting reassurance.

Finally, he ended his story with being shot, gesturing to where the bullet pierced him.

For the first time, he had managed to shock her, and she let out an audible gasp. Ellie moved her hand up, trying to find the scar.

"Here." He placed her fingers on his shirt over where he had been shot. She slinked under the fabric, finding the scar. Just a few inches below his heart.

"Ouch. That is not on my bucket list." While she was attempting to joke, her voice pitched with emotion in the middle.

Her soft fingers continued their stroking up and down under his shirt and he hissed, "Ellie." It was a warning. His self-control was unraveling in every passing moment.

She withdrew her hand, and he missed the comfort immediately. Instead, he pulled her even tighter to his side.

"The military, huh?" she finally murmured. "My best friend was in the military. I wonder if you met him."

Him? Maddox's anger peaked.

"Oliver, in fact. This is our go-to bar." She glanced down at her phone that had been buzzing for quite some time. "Looks like he tracked my location, again. The overprotective man is on his way. I apologize in advance for his uncouth behavior."

Maddox was practically seething, he barely heard her. The man tracked her? The man held her when she was touch-starved? Who was this man?

"Welp, here we go," Ellie mumbled dramatically.

"Isobel Rachelle Kane." The voice was familiar, and Maddox tried to identify the man covered in shadows that just walked into the bar.

"Oliver Jullian McKell," Ellie responded.

Maddox stiffened. It couldn't be. This could not be that *Isobel.*

The man stepped out of the shadows and met Maddox's eyes. "Maddox, what are you doing here?"

Maddox didn't expect for her best friend to also be the man that suggested this bar to him.

Fuck.

Maddox hadn't left Ellie's side since that day. He and Oliver came to an understanding. An agreement. Maddox wouldn't take her from Oliver, and Oliver would allow Maddox in her orbit. It didn't take long for Ellie to agree to him as her driver, and while that was his official title... Unofficially? He watched over her and kept her safe, as best he could. He still blamed himself for Harry. He took the night off to visit the grave of the girl he couldn't save.

When he came back the next day, it was already too late, and he knew better than to tell Ellie what to do. Harry had attached to her like the parasite he was.

Maddox wanted to force Ellie to see reason, but he would never take her choice away. He would never force anything on Ellie that she wasn't ready for. That she couldn't handle.

Eventually Maddox furthered his agreement with Oliver. Maddox knew Oliver was as obsessed with the girl as he was. Maddox understood he would never be able to be with her and keep her happy without Oliver.

And so, their plan was born. Ready Ellie to take them both. To have them both.

Together.

Chapter 12

Izzy

This was a mistake. In my top ten worst decisions I have ever made, hands down. That includes dry shaving my vagina while drunk as shit. It includes shot-gunning three energy drinks back-to-back before a funeral.

The only decision it was not worse than?

The day I followed my math teacher onto the school's roof.

"I'm ready to go," I whined to Oliver for the umpteenth time. We currently sat in our old high school gym which was honestly fancier than it had any right being. It was decked out in golden streamers, white satin clothed tables and chairs, and sparkling centerpieces. There was a dance floor in the middle where my old classmates grinded to early 2000s songs.

Hallie was on said dance floor, and Harry was shoving his dick into her asshole. Again. This time they at least had a smidgen of clothes on.

I turned in disgust and found Maddox's eyes on me. "What about you and I leave this popsicle stand and go rub one out in the principal's office."

Maddox choked. "Ellie."

"Yeah, yeah, I know. You two are off limits. Consider myself properly friendzoned." I was being a brat, but in my defense, I was currently living out a nightmare.

"Isobel." Oliver's voice was soft, and it felt too close to pity.

"You know what, *you-*" I pointed to Oliver "-find us some more clients. And *you-*" I turned my wrath on Maddox "-stop making the girls cry."

Though really, it was lowkey hilarious to watch him turn down boob job Betsy and her friend Polly. They were bullies in high school, and I couldn't help the satisfaction of watching him put them in their place now.

I grabbed my plastic cup of champagne and dramatically exited our table, going out to *mingle*. Honestly, I just wanted to stay off Sebastian York's radar. My teacher. The man that single handedly attempted to ruin my life. To take what wasn't his.

And even more so? I wanted to find an entirely different man. My third *friend* from high school that I hadn't seen or spoken to in 10 years. I doubted he would even be here, but I could hope. Would he even acknowledge me?

I placed a hand on my now rapidly beating heart, before chugging the champagne, and dropping the empty cup into the nearest trash station.

Five steps later and I somehow ended up in front of our old football captain, James.

James clearly peaked in high school, but who was I to tell him that? "Annabelle." Of course he would call me by the wrong name. The main bully that tormented me relentlessly in high school. The one that had caused more tears to shed than I cared to admit. Looking at him now, I'm embarrassed of my teenage self. Of crying over a schmuck like him.

"Jeremy." I returned the favor.

"My name is James."

"Cool, anyways I will just be going."

He grabbed my shoulder, stopping me and I watched his eyes peruse my body. I shivered disgustedly.

He licked his lips. "You were chubby in high school, but damn girl those curves, you sure grew into them."

"Looks like you didn't grow into yours." I attempted to escape his grip, but his fingers tightened.

"That's not very nice, I was trying to take pity on you. I'm a *nice* guy."

"Clearly." I reached up to remove his hand and practice some of my self-defense classes when a voice behind me had me stiffening.

"Now Mr. Lewis, this isn't how you treat women."

James mumbled an apology, dropping his hand and leaving me to the devil himself.

The man I was trying my best to avoid.

Mr. York; my senior year calculus teacher.

Chapter 13

Izzy

I was startled further when I settled my gaze on him, he looked... Different. I wouldn't recognize the man before me if it weren't for his voice. It was unmistakable. The soothing tone once comforted me when I was at my lowest. I fell into it. I believed he was just a kind man.

That wasn't the case at all.

"Mr. York," I greeted stiffly. I forced myself to push down my emotions. It was a technique I used to compartmentalize the parts of my life that were poisoned by this man. He was the reason I learned self-defense, why I left this town and never looked back, why I couldn't fly unless I was ten sheets to the wind.

He would not be the reason I broke down. I wouldn't allow him any more power than he already had.

"Now Bel, you know I told you to call me Sebastian."

The man stepped closer to me. He reached out, sweeping some of my hair behind my ear. I was frozen in place.

In high school, he dressed immaculately. He always wore thick-framed glasses that hid the color of his eyes and kept his hair shaved close to his scalp. Now?

He dressed in a leather jacket and all his uncovered skin was adorned in intricate tattoos. His black hair was touched in gray and fell in waves around his face. His charcoal eyes were on full display without any lenses obscuring their view. He was objectively handsome, but I knew better. His entire aura was opaque, shrouded in darkness. This was not a nice man.

"They allow you to teach like this?" I settled on the words. My legs began to once more function, allowing me to take a step back and put space between us.

Sebastian's eyes tracked my movement like the predator he was. "I quit ten years ago. Worked with my family, and then I moved. Where is your dearest Yara?"

I gulped audibly and glanced around, trying to find Maddox or Oliver, but I couldn't locate either. My emotions were trying to prickle up but I stamped them back down. "Sick. Where did you move to?" I continued the conversation without much thought, contemplating an exit strategy from this man.

"Sorry to hear that about Yara." A mockingly solicitous expression slid across his face. "I recently moved to New York."

My eyes shot to his. "Where in New York?" I asked shakily.

Sebastian's face darkened further, his eyes turned to infinite soulless canyons. "You know where."

Surely, he didn't. He couldn't have found and followed me. Suddenly, I felt entirely too exposed. My eyes landed on Hallie. Fuck. I caught her gaze and waved. This time, I was ready when a hand tried to stop me, and I dodged him as I beelined it to my step-sister.

"Izzy, there you are. No hard feelings, right? Sometimes men just need a little less to hold onto." Hallie wasted no time in her verbal assault, but for once I was grateful for her presence.

Sebastian preferred operating in the shadows, he would not want to make a scene. "No hard feelings," I agreed. "Harry," I acknowledged his existence. He didn't deserve it, but I needed to use their company until I could find Maddox or Oliver.

"Bel, I'm sorry, you know I still love you. If you want to talk to me, I am always here for you."

The cheating pig's voice was reminiscent of grinding brakes. I shivered disgustedly at the nickname. I had told him multiple times not to use it. I found myself once more questioning my sanity. And my choice in men.

"Thanks," I responded emotionlessly.

"You still love her? You didn't say that last night!" Hallie shrilled, but I finally spotted Maddox and paid them no mind.

"Well best of luck to you both." I did not wait for a response, before heading to Maddox. A hand on my wrist had me jerking to a stop and an eerily familiar man was holding my phone. What the fuck? It had been in my bag the entire night. Which was, of course, somehow now unzipped. And what was with everyone manhandling me?

"You dropped this." I followed the phone up and up and up to a pair of hooded caramel eyes.

I yanked my wrist free from his calloused fingers and grabbed my phone. I searched for a name tag on the mystery man but didn't see one. I didn't have the patience or energy to put anymore into this interaction, even if he was sexy as hell and hauntingly familiar. Especially his eyes. "Thanks." I murmured the word, before continuing my path to Maddox. I felt the strange man's intense stare on me the entirety of my retreat.

When I was finally within Maddox's reach, I pushed myself into his arms. "I need to leave. Butterscotch."

Maddox stiffened. "What happened? Are you okay?"

"Those aren't the rules." Butterscotch was the word I could use to leave a situation with no questions asked.

Maddox gave me an indiscernible look but wrenched out his cell phone and typed out a message furiously. "Let's go, Oliver knows we're leaving."

I gave one more backwards look to the towering man with the caramel eyes. I was shocked to see he was still watching me. He raised his hand and brought a finger to his lips before disappearing out of sight.

Confusion swept through me as a chill crept across my skin, but it wasn't in fear. It was something else entirely.

Chapter 14

Oliver

His Isobel

The man from the plane was here. The fake name he had on all his traveling documents made it difficult for Milo to track his movements, but right as Oliver received the text from Maddox, Oliver spotted him.

Watching his Isobel.

Oliver continued to survey his surroundings and found another man he didn't know also focused on Isobel's retreat.

What. The. Fuck.

He cursed; this was a horrible decision. He should have just let her stay at the hotel with Maddox. He hoped this reunion would make her realize how much better she was than all these fools, not throw her in the direction of more unsavory men.

"Ollie." A shrill whining voice brought his attention back to the disgusting woman in front of him. He tried to relocate both of the men watching *his* Isobel but could no longer spot either in the growing crowd of drunken alumni.

"Yes dear, here is my card. If you ever need our services let us know." He pushed it to her distractedly. He couldn't recall the girl's name and, as with most of the guests, she opted not to wear a nametag.

"Can I sample the services now?" A fake fingernail dug along Oliver's skin, and he did his best to contain his rage.

She was exactly the type of person that he hated. A rodent dressed in nice clothes and filled with plastic was still a rodent.

He jerked back and gave her a faux smile. "Sorry dear, I must be on my way."

The rat went to touch him again, but he was already spinning and disappearing into the crowd. He needed to join his Isobel. And he needed to make sure these two men here wouldn't be a problem.

Chapter 15

Izzy

I was finally alone. It took all sorts of threatening, but Maddox eventually left my hotel room. With the promise of being only feet away.

Yara was no longer destroying my toilet, so I sent her a quick text.

Me: *You good?*

Yara: *Better. I'll know if you bail. You didn't take it earlier, but don't worry, check under your pillow <3*

I threw my phone down onto the ground dramatically and walked to the pillows.

Come to Bed stared back at me in bold red print on the manila folder.

One more glance to the adjoining door and I jerked the folder up and walked to my bathroom, locking the door. Neither Maddox nor Oliver knew what personal space was.

Thankfully there was no indication of the massacre that Yara put the toilet through earlier, and I was able to breathe without the smell of vomit souring the space. Now it just smelled of bleach.

Feeling secure, I leaned against the sink counter and opened the folder. A pen and room key fell out and I scooped them from the ground.

The room key matched the one I had for my current room. The number was different, but it was on the same floor.

I sucked in a deep breath.

The top page was the NDA. I scanned it before signing.

Placing the NDA on the counter, I turned to the next page.

I pushed the air out aggressively. I was really doing this. No turning back now.

Welcome to your Darkest Desires

IF YOU ARE READING THIS, YOU HAVE FINALLY TAKEN THE PLUNGE TO SATISFY YOUR NEEDS.

CONGRATULATIONS. WE ARE PROUD OF YOU. THERE IS NO NEED TO FEEL SHAME.

YOUR SATISFACTION AND SAFETY ARE OUR TOP PRIORITIES. ON THE NEXT PAGE YOU WILL CONFIRM WE HAVE CORRECTLY MARKED YOUR BOUNDARIES. WE WANT TO ENSURE THAT NOTHING GOES AWRY.

THERE WILL BE A PLACE TO PUT YOUR SAFEWORD. THIS WORD WILL BE USED BY YOUR PARTNER, OR PARTNERS, AS WELL.

IF YOU HAVE SELECTED TO KNOW YOUR PARTNER PRIOR, YOU WILL RECEIVE THEIR SUMMARY BELOW.

IF YOU HAVE SELECTED TO GO INTO THIS BLIND, YOU WILL NOT BE PROVIDED WITH ANY OF THEIR INFORMATION, BUT PLEASE REST ASSURED THAT THEY ARE A MATCH FOR YOU.

YOUR PARTNER, OR PARTNERS, HAVE BEEN THOROUGHLY VETTED AND TESTED. THEY WENT THROUGH THE SAME PROCESS YOU DID.

WE HOPE THIS TURNS INTO EXACTLY WHAT YOU WISH IT TO BE.

I scrunched up my brow. Should I have asked to see the man first? Maybe. But I trusted Yara, and I needed this. I required something to get Sebastian out of my mind. To stomp down my growing lust for both Oliver and Maddox. Maybe this was exactly what I needed. I flipped the page.

Boundaries

PLEASE NOTE THAT THIS IS NOT A COMPLETE LIST, THIS IS ONLY WHAT WAS INPUT ON YOUR PROFILE. IF YOU HAVE ANYTHING SPECIFICALLY YOU WISH FOR YOUR PARTNER(S) TO PARTICIPATE IN, PLEASE CIRCLE IT ON THIS PAGE. YOU CAN REQUEST YOUR PARTNER(S) COMPLETE SOMETHING NOT LISTED, BUT THAT IS AT THEIR DISCRETION. ANY ITEMS ON THE DENIED LIST WILL BE RESPECTED.

ACCEPTED

- USING SEX TOYS, VIBRATORS OR DILDOS, WITH A PARTNER
- SOAKING AFTER INTERCOURSE
- BUTT PLUGS
- BLINDFOLDS
- SLEEP PLAY
- ANAL INTERCOURSE
- VAGINAL INTERCOURSE
- ORAL SEX, VAGINAL
- BITING
- SPANKING
- ROLEPLAY—CNC
- ROLEPLAY—FORCED BREEDING

UNSURE

- MULTIPLE PARTNERS
- SHIBARI
- CROPS

DENIED

- FISTING
- ELECTROSTIMULATION
- DVP
- DAP

SAFEWORD:____________________________________

ADDITIONAL INFORMATION:____________________________

My face turned progressively redder as I scanned through the list. I input most of it onto my profile over a year ago, but some I had added more recently. We were forced to write in our own words what it was that we wanted and didn't want. I was sure there was more I needed to add to the denied list, but my stream of missionary partners hadn't done much to allow me to dive into the kink community.

I had always been interested in it and I always felt something was missing. My excitement grew as I realized I was finally going to live out a fantasy.

I scribbled down my go-to safeword. BUTTERSCOTCH. I circled one singular request above. It was something I had always wanted to try, but never felt comfortable enough to ask my previous partners.

Sleep play. Or as the internet had so helpfully informed me: *dormaphilia*.

Sleep play was giving consent to something otherwise non-consensual. I wanted someone else in control because I allowed them to be, not because they chose to be. It felt like taking back the script. The thought of it made me feel powerful.

I wanted the man to use me exactly how he wanted, but only because I allowed it. I desired to be pushed to my limits with the ability to stop it. I needed to be forced out of my comfort zone with a safe partner.

My stomach fluttered uncomfortably with moths desperately trying to escape, but I ignored it.

I was ready.

Chapter 16
Izzy

It was time. I took a picture of my signed NDA and my finalized form, uploading it to my profile and sending a copy to Yara, too.

I folded the form to bring with me and left the rest in the folder hidden underneath my mattress. I dressed in my favorite Mumu and feigned illness to Oliver and Maddox.

"Just leave me be!" I yelled at them both standing guard at our adjoining room's door. I knew they were both worried from earlier, but we could get into that later.

I already had enough anxiety about this without their mother hen energy mucking up the place.

"You sure you don't need anything?" Oliver's tone was saturated with worry, and I immediately felt guilty for lying to him. To them both. But they would never let me do this.

"I'll be fine, just let me rest please."

They both offered up uneasy smiles before exiting my room and closing the door behind them.

I sent out a blank text to Yara. It was her signal.

A few minutes later, I heard them exiting their room. I wasn't sure how she convinced the overprotective men away from me, but I didn't waste any more time.

I threw a robe over my sleepwear, grabbed the form with my request, both hotel keys, stepped into my slippers, and exited my room. I felt like I was a teenager sneaking out as I glanced both ways before making my way down the hall. While the room was on the same floor, it was two hallways away.

When I made it, I breathed a sigh of relief as the door *slunk* shut behind me. The room was identical to the one I was staying in, except this one had clearly not been used yet.

Walking fully into the space, I emptied the pockets of my robe on the bedside table and eyed the bottle of wine there. I plucked the card that was placed at the bottom, reading it.

Cheers to satisfying your desires.

I could get behind that. Thankfully it was a twist top and I made quick work of opening it. I swiftly filled and threw back a glass before shedding my robe and getting comfortable in the bed.

Nervous energy was coursing through me, but the alcohol was doing its job.

Sleep play was something I had read about and always wanted to try, but this was all very new.

What if I just thought I would like it? What if I ended up hating every moment?

Even though I wanted this, I was still so anxious. I reached over and plucked the wine from the bedside table, taking a swig straight from the bottle this time. I set it down after several large gulps.

It was time.

I adjusted my Mumu and closed my eyes. I did my best to calm my breathing and fall asleep, because I knew when I woke up, it would be to a man inside of me.

Chapter 17

Maddox

His Ellie

"Where the fuck is she?" Oliver raged as they entered Ellie's room. Oliver had the cameras in her bedroom hooked up to his phone and Maddox watched as Oliver rewound until it showed Isobel exiting. Moments after Yara called for their assistance.

Maddox was livid, but he needed to keep calm. "Maybe she went for medicine?"

Oliver continued his rampage. "Isobel's phone is showing it's here. Why would she leave without it?" Oliver began throwing everything off of her bed, in the process the mattress was moved, and Maddox spotted something amiss.

Maddox stepped forward grabbing the folder. "Call. Yara. Now!" he spat out.

Come to Bed. Stared back at him as he furiously opened the folder. Dread sunk deep into his gut. He knew what this was, but he desperately wanted to be wrong.

The signed NDA stared up at him. He threw it to the ground and read the first line of the next page, before letting loose a snarl.

Welcome to your Darkest Desires

"I am going to kill her. I am going to murder Yara. I will strangle her with my bare hands." Maddox's voice was icy and cold.

Oliver stopped his destruction of her room, Ellie's phone in his hand. "I missed her texting Yara, that was a distraction. Why?"

"Look at this." Maddox held the sheet up to Oliver.

"Yara is going to die," Oliver confirmed.

They were once more on the same page, but first? They needed to find their girl before this unknown chump touched what was theirs.

Chapter 18

James Lewis

James left the reunion an hour prior and had wasted no time pounding shots back-to-back at their local sports bar. He was stewing on his interaction with Annabelle. That fat girl thought she was better than him? Well, she fucking wasn't, and he was planning on picking up the first piece of ass that gave him the eyes.

The alcohol eventually caught up with him and James moved towards the bathroom, to find the door locked and an out of order sign adorning it. He jiggled the handle a few more times, but it didn't give way.

Cursing, James tried the woman's restroom and found the exact same sign and situation.

Fed up, he made his way out the back door to the alley behind the bar and unzipped his jeans. He began doing his business against the dumpster that was placed between the bar and the end of the alley.

The door behind him slamming open had his stream jerking and landing on his shoes.

"Fuck, what the fuck man?" James hurriedly tucked his dick away and turned around ready to start an altercation with whoever interrupted.

Only to feel a piercing burn in his chest, James' eyes flew downwards to watch as a knife continued its path into his body.

A gloved hand pushing it into place.

James eyes stayed open just long enough to make out his murderer.

"You?" he expelled hoarsely as the knife was removed and he fell to the ground.

The weapon dripped with crimson as James shook aggressively and took his last shallow breaths.

"One down, two to go." Were the last words James ever heard, before he shuddered one final time, collapsing face up on his own piss in the alley way.

Lifeless.

Chapter 19

Izzy

I felt wet. Sensual. Something was pushing into me. My hips rolled on their own accord into the feeling.

"That's a good girl, let me stretch you," a dark voice rasped out as he pushed his fingers into me forcefully. It felt *incredible*.

I teetered on the line of consciousness, my eyes still firmly shut. I allowed myself to just feel, without thought. A vibration found my clit and I moaned into my pillow.

"Yes, you are almost ready for me," the same deep voice continued, "I need to taste you, but first I need *you*. I've waited too long."

The words echoed around my sleep-addled brain as I slowly came into consciousness. Before I could open my eyes, I was flipped onto my hands and knees by rough, strong hands and dragged to the edge of the bed. A few moments later, something silky was placed over my eyes, covering them.

"We'll do this again, I promise. But this time, fall into the sensations."

I was still not fully awake, and I allowed my diluted mind to accept the man's suggestion. This was an ethereal encounter. I was falling into the feelings and not allowing my rationale to cloud the experience.

The man repositioned himself. He now seemed to stand on the ground, while I was on my hands and knees on the edge of the bed. I felt the vibrations return to my clit as, simultaneously, something much larger than his fingers pushed at my entrance.

He had already gotten me to the edge before I became aware of it. My body reacting to what my mind was just now catching up on. I could feel tingling between my thighs, my muscles clenching up, and I was *hot*. I could tell he had been using the vibrator on me as I slept, and I was *close*.

I whimpered as he continued pressing into me, stretching me. It was too much. I wasn't sure he would fit. "Too big." The words were garbled as I was pushed face first into the bed. Contrary to my words, my desire increased, and tension began to curl even tighter deep inside. I was loving every moment of this.

Of my lack of control.

"That's not the word," the man grunted out harshly before slamming completely into me.

I came on a scream, convulsing around his thick cock. I fought him, but one of his large hands used my hip as a handle to hold me in place. I was officially fully awake.

"What a good, dirty girl, you take me so well." He leaned over my back kissing and sucking on my neck while pulling the vibrator away.

I relaxed slowly, allowing myself to adjust to his size.

Was that it? I did come, but I wasn't sure what to expect next. Right when I thought he was just going to pull out and end it there, he pushed the vibrator up once more finding my clit.

I needed more of him.

"Hold this," he commanded.

I reached down holding the vibrator in place over my sensitive clit. "It's too much," I whined.

Long calloused fingers stroked the back of my hand before pulling away.

I wasn't sure if I could take much more of this. Even in my anxiety, I couldn't help but love every moment with this man. I was overwhelmed in both the worst and best kind of way, and I was *enjoying* it. The thought caught me off guard. I never realized how deeply I needed this experience.

I was his to fuck. I allowed it. This was my choice.

"You're going to need it." That was the only warning I got before he set a brutal pace. He used his other, now free, hand to hold me by the back of my neck. His long fingers wrapped to the front and squeezed with just the right pressure, causing jolts of desire.

"Fuck," I expelled out another moan. I was unraveling. Everything about this man was stripping me bare and I couldn't even see him.

But he overwhelmed my remaining senses. His words, his voice, his smell, his strength.

His domination.

That's what he was doing: dominating my body. Ruining me for any future missionary encounters.

He lifted me up off the bed and used my body to lift and drop me down his length, hitting a spot inside I wasn't aware existed. Every time he hit it, I let out a tiny gasp.

I never wanted this to end.

It didn't take long for the tension to pool once more. "Fuck, fuck, *fuck*!" I gasped out. He was everywhere. He engulfed me. I needed more and less of him at the same time. I was drowning in the endless pleasure and yet I felt as if I could never get enough of it.

"Yes, take me. All of it." He pushed my face back into the bed and pulled all the way out before slamming back in.

"No more!" I sobbed as I contracted once more around his length. I wasn't sure if I actually meant the words this time. He was in control of this encounter, but even still, I felt safe. I knew inherently that he would stop if I spoke my safeword.

That I was ultimately the one in control.

I felt heat fill me as he came. "You're going to take every drop of my cum and keep it in that cunt of yours." He pulled out for just a moment before flipping me over and pushing back inside.

I needed to see his face. See who had ruined me.

I went to take the blindfold off, but he caught my hands.

"Not this time. Tomorrow night. Same time? Whatever you want."

The fact that he felt the same way? That he wanted to do this again? I felt my cheeks flush.

I hummed my agreement. He could ask for anything at this moment and I might just agree. I felt as he lifted me up from the bed and repositioned us so I was straddling him, his dick still inside. Typically, my self-conscious side would shine when I was on a man, but I could tell he was sturdy. His bulk was almost too much for me to wrap my legs around.

Muscular arms enveloped my body and his crisp tangy scent invaded my being. I could practically taste him. He smelled comfortingly familiar. Of a good memory I couldn't quite place.

His hands reached down to cup me under the curve of my ass in a gentle hold. His strong fingers stroked my skin, leaving scalding fire in their wake. He held me like that for a long time in comfortable silence—just the beating of our hearts—before he finally disentangled our bodies, laying me down gently as he got up. I left the blindfold in place, even though I wanted more than anything to see this man.

A few minutes later a warm cloth began cleaning me. "Go back to sleep, little one. Pick something for us to do tomorrow night, and I promise not to disappoint."

"Mmm," I mumbled out. I allowed the man to sit me up and felt as my Mumu fell over my form.

The soft material was a comfort against my bruised skin. I expected the man to leave right away, but he didn't. Instead, he tugged my back to his chest and held me in his arms.

I ignored my insecurity that bubbled up with his arms wrapped around my stomach and permitted myself to fall into his embrace.

"You are perfection, little one, now go to sleep. I promise to come for you again." The man's hot breath on my neck left goosebumps in their wake.

I snuggled back, deeper into the security of his arms. He was providing the aftercare I didn't even know I so desperately craved.

I once more did my best to fall asleep.

This time wasn't nearly as difficult.

Yara was right, I needed this. I needed this man.

I hadn't felt this satisfied in years. This comfortable. This completely at ease.

And I had every intention of doing it again.

And again.

And *again*.

Chapter 20
Oliver
His Isobel

She had been missing for six hours.

Six hours.

Oliver paced their room frantically; he was long since past the point of rational thought. Yara decided it best to get on a flight leaving shortly after being used as a distraction. If Yara weren't already halfway back home to California. She would be dead.

"Milo found the room." Maddox's words broke through Oliver's inner plans of premeditated murder. "There's something else too."

Oliver glanced at the message Maddox received and cursed, one problem at a time though.

"Her room is on this floor? Are you fucking kidding me?" Oliver marched out of theirs and down the hallway continuing his rampage until he found the one, she was in, he didn't wait for Maddox. He kicked the door open in one attempt.

His Isobel shot up from the bed.

Oliver took less than a moment to investigate her surroundings. He was towering over her in five seconds. Ten seconds later she was over his shoulder. Sixty seconds after that, he was tossing her onto his bed back in his room.

"What the fuck?" Isobel seethed. "I was perfectly fine."

Maddox stepped into the room, ended his call, and joined Oliver at his side. "Hotel has been notified of an accident. We will be left alone." Maddox turned his attention to Isobel. "What have you done?"

"You two both keep forgetting I am a grown adult! I can be out of your sight for more than a day without you calling the fucking bomb squad. I don't need this!" Isobel went to get up, but it was too late. She wouldn't be leaving this room anytime soon.

Oliver's hands shot out keeping her on the bed and he watched as her sleep dress rode up, exposing her swollen pussy. "Who touched you? What did you do?" Oliver's worry and rage redirected to Isobel. He snatched her sleep dress off her body and took in the sight of her.

Hickeys adorned the left side of her neck. Bruises lined her hips and neck, the clear indentation of fingers. He saw red.

"What the fuck!?" Isobel screeched attempting to cover herself. "You aren't the boss of me!"

Oliver's dick jerked in his pants. Anytime she called him boss, it riled him up.

Oliver knew another man had been inside her hours prior, but he didn't care. It was time. He gave Maddox a nod and Maddox returned it. They began to strip.

"What is going on? I need to shower and get dressed!" Isobel continued to fight against Oliver, but he held her wrists in one hand and finished unbuttoning his pants with the other.

"We wanted to wait until you were ready, but you forced our hand. Do you understand me?" His pants now pushed to the ground, he brought his free hand to her face, squeezing it.

"What is going on? Is this some sort of joke?" Isobel's typical ferocity turned unsure.

Maddox walked in just his boxers to the bed on the opposite side. "You are ours. No more other men. Do you understand me?"

Isobel jerked in Oliver's grip, turning to face Maddox. "No, I really don't understand. I get that you both are angry, but you're going a bit far." Her voice now quivered with uncertainty.

"We are not going 'a bit far', do you not understand what you do to me? To both of us? How much it hurts every time you allow another shithead into your life? Enough is enough, Ellie. I wanted to give you time to understand on your own, to realize that all you needed was right before your eyes." Maddox paused to let out a heavy shuddering breath. He stroked the side of her face in a soft caress.

Oliver watched the interaction, he suspected his jealousy might bubble up, but it didn't. Instead, his dick turned to steel.

"But you are so incredibly dense! You are the most sexy, confident woman I know, except when it comes to men. When it comes to us especially. So, no Ellie we are not going 'a bit far'. In fact, we haven't gone nearly far enough." On that last note, Maddox reached forward and in one fell swoop slipped his fingers into Isobel's cunt. "It seems the last man left something behind. I'll have to fix that."

Isobel's mouth formed an O and Oliver shoved her back on the bed, she was only halfway up, and her legs dangled off the end. The sight had Oliver's throat drying. His imagination was nothing compared to this. The images through a screen couldn't compare. His Isobel laid bare in their control? Fuck. He was past ready. He needed her.

"You have five seconds to stop this. We know your safeword." Maddox warned her, freeing his already erect dick from his boxers and positioning himself.

"Stop what? My safeword? Why would I need to use that? You haven't explained anything. What do you mean I need to open my eyes? I thought you both friendzoned—" Maddox cut her off by slamming his dick into her open mouth.

"Time's up sweetheart, now listen close." Oliver spoke the words while pushing her face up and squeezing her mouth open for Maddox's cock to continue his furious strokes into her mouth. "You have always looked up to me, I know you did. You think I am some perfect man, but I'm not. I never have been. I am a selfish man, I kept you as close to me as I possibly could. I track your phone, I watch you through those cameras you installed, I follow your every move. You are my obsession, *Isobel*. You're lucky that Maddox came along to help me with my self-control, otherwise you would have been locked away years ago. Away from the world's, and every other man's, prying eyes. I hope you learn that quickly, because once I have you this one time, there will be no escaping me again. I will be imprinted in your skin. In every breath you take. In every movement you make. It will be because I allowed you to. But I can promise you one thing, while you may be my obsession, I am your servant."

Tears slowly formed in Isobel's eyes, and she began to struggle, Maddox pulled out to allow her a few moments of breath before he invaded her, choking her again.

"You are ours. We let you go out and have your fun, but this was too far. You went too far. So now? You're going to take us both." Oliver snarled the last of his words out, shedding the rest of his clothes and gripping his cock in his hand.

Maddox once more withdrew from Isobel's swollen lips allowing her another moment to breathe.

The confusion and shock on Isobel's face slowly morphed to understanding. "Cameras? My room? I thought you were just keeping me safe. I didn't realize, I never knew." She looked between the men. "Why didn't either of you tell me? Why hadn't you said anything before?" She was eerily calm in her questions. "Maddox, we kissed? Oliver, you know I had a crush on you. Why did you wait all this time?"

Oliver's face turned almost menacing. "You weren't ready. Do you think if we told you this years ago, you would have accepted this? Allowed us both to touch you like this? I may not be a good man, but I only wanted you if you were willing. If you were ready."

"I guess...I guess not," Isobel stuttered the words, but she wasn't trying to run and escape.

Oliver watched her carefully, she may not notice it, but she was slowly leaning into both the men.

"That doesn't explain you though, Maddox."

Maddox grunted, "We made an agreement. If we had not, Oliver would not have allowed me in your orbit."

Oliver shrugged. "He's not wrong. But now here we are exactly where we want you. We can figure out the rest later. For now? I've waited long enough; I refuse to wait any longer."

His Isobel still seemed confused, but a slow sultry smile graced her face. "Okay, whatever this is, let's do it. But you promise to stop if it's too much?"

Oliver could not contain himself and he leaned down pushing his lips to hers. "We promise."

"Of course, baby girl, I would never do anything you didn't want." Maddox bent down and picked up a piece of paper that had fallen to the floor. "But look what I found in that room, what a naughty Ellie. It appears there's quite a bit you *do* want."

Oliver snatched the paper from Maddox's hand and as he read a sinister grin grew on his lips. "Seems we're going to have to test those boundaries."

Chapter 21
Maddox
His Ellie

Repositioning, Maddox allowed Ellie just a moment to see what he was doing, before he pushed his dick through her lips. The feel of Ellie's hot mouth around Maddox's cock had him using all of his self-control not to fuck into her with ruthless abandon.

It was better than he imagined, not only how she felt, but the ability to have her in his control. Exactly where he wanted her.

To finally tell her what he had wanted to, all those years ago. That he would never be leaving her side. That he was there to stay.

Ellie's teeth lightly scraped the tip of his head, and he hissed as shockwaves of pleasure rolled through him. She did it again, and he tangled his hand in her hair, forcing himself deeper down her throat. When he thought he hit her limit, she surprised him by pushing forward a bit more and swallowing around him.

Maddox growled at her, "Fuck Ellie!"

Maddox's desire surged as she continued to undo his loosening hold on his self-control and right as the dam broke, he withdrew, leaving his tip just centimeters from her face. Ropes of his cum coated her eyelashes and mouth. He gave her a feral grin.

He loved leaving his mark on her.

Ellie was finally accepting what was going on and he watched her relax into it as Maddox used his discarded shirt to wipe her clean.

"Fuck. You know how much I care about you both don't you? What are we even doing? What if this ruins everything?" Ellie panted, her cheeks red and eyes watering.

He needed more.

"There will be time for talking later, but I promise we aren't going anywhere, no matter what," Oliver replied matter-of-factly. "We know your safeword, but Isobel? We both know you won't be using it."

Ellie gulped audibly and Maddox watched the movement in a trance. He needed to be back inside her, he exchanged a look with Oliver. Once more on the same page, they rearranged Ellie together ignoring her protests as they manhandled her. She was now on her hands and knees between them. Maddox found his dick was already almost ready to go again and gave it a few more strokes using her saliva as lubricant. He knew he would never get enough of her.

"This *unsure* on multiple partners?" Oliver's tone was mocking, and his dick was at Ellie's lips while Maddox was on his knees behind her. "We're going to fix that." Oliver squeezed her mouth open and used his grip to thrust into it.

Maddox did not waste any time, even though he wanted nothing more than to slam into her, he needed to prepare her first. He laid down under the junction of her thighs and pulled her down onto his face. He didn't care of the mess the other man left behind. He would just have to fill her up himself.

He focused on Ellie. On her taste, her sounds, her intoxicating smell. Floral and sweet.

She made a startled noise, trying to lift away from Maddox's mouth.

He lifted his hand up spanking her. "Let me taste you!" His deep voice vibrating against her cunt.

Maddox used Oliver's rhythm to set his own as he licked her up and down. She began to squirm, and Maddox brought his hand up to push a finger into her cunt. She gasped around Oliver's dick. She tried to wiggle away again, but he used his other hand to hold onto her hip bone, to keep her firmly in place. It was his favorite handle. "That's it baby girl, you're almost ready."

She was everything. He couldn't wait to be inside her. Claiming her.

He pushed in another finger and bit down onto her clit at the same time. She let out a whimpering noise and began to convulse around his fingers and he crooked them trying to find her favorite spots. "Oh, did you like that, Ellie? That's just the start of it, baby." Maddox promised.

From above Oliver grunted, "Fuck Isobel, you are magnificent."

Satisfied she was ready, and he would be able to make her come again, Maddox lifted her up off his face as Oliver withdrew from her mouth. A string of her saliva pulled from the tip of his dick to her lips. Maddox heard as she gulped down Oliver's cum. Maddox wiped her juices from his face and grinned ferociously at Oliver.

"First," Maddox snapped out, he wasn't waiting any longer. "You good?" he asked in a softer tone to Ellie.

A soft "More" was Ellie's only response, she turned her face back to him and he was pleased at how she looked. *Wrecked*.

Oliver didn't argue with Maddox, he instead bent down and kissed her on the lips passionately. With the distraction, Maddox lined up with her entrance and slowly began pushing his way inside. He guessed she might be sore, but her pliable body sucked him in.

"Fuck!" Maddox grunted out. He couldn't keep his gentle pace. "Rub her," he directed Oliver when he made it halfway.

Oliver didn't argue, he simply moved into place and began to swipe circles over her clit.

Ellie writhed and moaned, trying to once more escape him, but Maddox wouldn't allow it, with both hands on her hips he slammed the rest of the way into her. She felt incredible and it sent shockwaves through him. He set a bruising pace as Oliver helped push her to the edge.

"This is what you've always wanted isn't it? To be used by us both?" Maddox growled out as he continued pounding into her.

The garbled noises of pleasure continued to leave her, but in the midst, he heard a needy "Yes" bleed through.

Maddox spread her ass so he could push even further into her. It was his undoing, he felt as fire licked down his spine. The pressure swelled. "You're going to come again for me!" he commanded her.

Oliver now was playing with her pink nipples, rolling one into his mouth, as he worked her clit.

Maddox found a spot inside her that caused her to moan especially loudly, and he continued his rhythm pushing at it over. And over again.

After only a few more strokes into that spot, she came with a sultry scream. Maddox lasted just long enough for her to begin pulsating over his length before he was filling her.

He slowly, regretfully pulled out and Oliver gently tugged Ellie onto his chest. Maddox laid down next to the two, he reached his hand up to her cunt.

Ellie gasped, "What are you doing?"

Maddox pushed his come back into her, cupping her pussy, and keeping his hand there. "You weren't going to let any of this out, were you baby girl?"

She moaned softly into Oliver's chest. Oliver wrapped her in his arms and began stroking her back.

It wasn't long before Maddox heard her breath steady out, the unmistakable sound that she had fallen asleep. He kept his hand in place.

Warmth swelled in his chest; she trusted them no matter what they did.

Maddox and Oliver exchanged a look.

They weren't done yet, but she needed her rest.

Was it too soon to tell Ellie he loved her? Maddox hoped not, because he knew soon, the words would just spill out.

Chapter 22

Harry

Harry lay on his bed in his hotel room fisting his cock to a video he took of Bel when they first fucked. She wasn't aware of it which meant no harm, no foul.

Harry was pissed. She should have just stayed with him, so what if he fucked Hallie? It was just in her ass, does that even count? He was a catch and Bel was lucky to have him. There was enough of him to go around. But seriously, as long as he didn't have feelings for the other person, why did it matter? Stupid women.

He loved Bel, he told her that every day. He gave her everything she could ask for.

A knock at his door had him letting out an aggravated noise.

"Room service."

He had most certainly not ordered room service, but maybe it was some sort of apology from Hallie for fucking everything up. She promised him no strings attached in the message he received from her, but here she was trying to get him to *marry* her.

Harry had a ring, but it was reserved for Bel; he just needed to convince her to take him back. And he had just the plan.

Knock her up.

He tucked his cock in his pants and walked to the door. He swung it open, about to berate whoever it was, but before he could get anything out, a cart was pushed into him and he fell to the ground below.

He went to yell at his assailant, but hands covered his mouth and he felt something prick his arm.

Before he even had the time to panic, his entire body relaxed and he was no longer able to move at all.

He never saw his assailant, but he heard a rough voice as darkness began to shroud his vision.

"Two down, one more to go."

Harry closed his eyes for the last time.

Chapter 23

Izzy

"Mmmm," I moaned through my sleepy haze. Was I dreaming? I fell into the feelings, the touch, the trance.

"I'm going to fuck you. If you don't want me to, you better tell me soon." Oliver's unmistakable voice swam through the haze, but I paid it no mind.

This sex dream was everything I could ever, well, *dream* of. Fingers were pinching and massaging my nipples. They moved delightfully along my sides and slowly traced down, down, and down until they found my clit. They stopped there for just a moment, before continuing their path even further.

Finally, they pushed gently into my folds, but instead of applying the pressure I needed, they seemed to be lathering their fingers from the wetness that pooled between my thighs. I tried to push further into the touch, but I was held in place.

"No Isobel, I need to get you ready." Oliver's husky voice rolled down my neck, and I stopped my attempts to get the pressure I needed. I didn't want the dream to end.

"Baby girl, you really do like this don't you? So, fucking hot. She's so fucking wet." Maddox's gruff voice joined in my dream.

A moment later and the long fingers continued their path all the way to my ass. They pushed into the rim of muscle, the lubricant allowing them easy access. I had never had someone touch me there, only ever a toy. But another person? It was *everything*.

I rolled further onto it, I needed more. This felt *too* good.

"Fuck, she is ready. She's going to be able to take us both."

"Ellie, baby girl? We're going to fuck you. At the same time. Are you ready for that?" Maddox's voice was soft and husky.

"Yes, please," I murmured the words softly.

Another finger found its way to my clit, but the one in my ass slowly pulled out and I whimpered.

"More," I begged, my eyes still firmly shut. I was beginning to suspect this wasn't a dream, but I needed more, and I didn't want to ruin it.

Behind me I heard rustling. "I'm going to put a condom on before I fuck your ass. More lube, less clean up. Next time we can prepare you better, but I can't wait any longer. I know you've never been with anyone there before. And this virgin ass? It's mine." Oliver's tone darkened and I felt as something large pushed lightly in from behind. "Fuck!" he expelled the word.

I was awake now, this was reality. And I was loving every fucking moment of it. I kept my eyes shut, enjoying the need to rely on my other senses.

I could admit that I was fully a dormaphiliac. That I loved relinquishing control, and even more so? That I loved these two men's obsessions with me. However wrong it might be.

The slippery rubber of the condom made it easier, but he kept pushing and pushing and pushing into me, and I began to become anxious of when it would stop. How long was he? I had a toy I used, but it wasn't nearly this big. Right before I thought I might need to actually use my safeword, I felt his balls against my ass cheeks.

"Jesus fucking christ, you're so tight." He repositioned us and I let out a strangled noise as he laid me on him. My back on his chest. He pressed even further into me, the fingers on my clit never letting up.

Movement on the bed had me finally opening my eyes.

Maddox's face was a mask of lust, want, and need. He was gloriously naked and his large muscular frame was repositioning above us. "Are you ready?"

I wasn't sure who the question was for, but I nodded my head softly.

He used his hands to spread my legs and he slowly lowered himself onto me. Oliver's fingers took over on my clit as I was filled. Maddox's cock rubbed against Oliver's, only a thin layer separating the two. Maddox paused there watching my face carefully, he leaned down to kiss me and the movement pressed Oliver into my G-Spot. A sultry moan I barely recognized as my own left my lips. They were wrecking me. This was something I had only ever imagined.

Maddox gave a toothy smile before pressing his full lips to mine. He forced his way into my mouth and began to slowly thrust into me.

"My Isobel." Oliver's deep voice in my ear caused goosebumps to form across my body. His free large hand reached between Maddox and I and it began to cup and tease my breast.

Oliver allowed Maddox to set the beat for both the men as Maddox continued to lightly thrust into me. I bit his lip and he ended the kiss chuckling softly.

"Ferocious," Maddox appraised, before he began to pound into me with ruthless abandon.

I was so incredibly full, but I felt no pain as they stretched me to my limits.

Both men knew me better than I knew myself.

Gasps left me as each thrust pushed Oliver into my G-spot. The noises sent Maddox into a frenzy as he began to do hard long thrusts into me. He hit a place inside that caused my vision to blur and my nerves to tingle. It wasn't long before I was tipped back over the precipice, contracting around both of the men, in ecstasy.

Maddox continued his thrusts for a few more beats, before his cock convulsed deep inside me. He withdrew slowly, offering me a soft kiss, before allowing Oliver to finish himself off with my body.

Oliver held onto my ass cheeks as he popped us up and down on the bed from below.

I didn't even feel the typical self-consciousness. I was aware of Oliver's strength. That my weight was nothing to him.

Maddox's fingers found his way inside to the mess he left behind and he pushed against Oliver's cock.

Oliver hissed below me in my ear, and I felt his length jerk up as he came.

Maddox's teeth nipped at my clit and the mixture of sensations caused an unexpected orgasm to rock through me.

It felt different than I was used to; I had never had two back-to-back like that.

Maddox removed his fingers sitting back on the bed. Watching me intently.

"You are everything and better than I could possibly imagine," Oliver whispered the sweet words into my ear as he rolled us and gently pulled out of me. I heard him get up, when he returned he tugged me into his arms. Wrapping me in his embrace from behind. Maddox did the same from the front. Cocooning me. I lifted my hands up and played softly with the curls of hair on Maddox's chest.

It was a heady feeling. Being used and abused by the two men I knew would do anything to keep me safe. That had sworn their loyalty to me.

That I trusted with every fabric of my being.

It wasn't long before the two men's breathing evened out and they fell asleep, but it was taking me a bit longer.

I already loved both of the men, I was already halfway *in* love with them both too if I was being truly honest with myself. It was something I had always inherently known but kept buried as an impossibility. I was still worried that when the dust settled, they would decide that this wasn't what they wanted after all. That I wasn't who they thought I was.

The imposter syndrome was one I was incredibly familiar with.

And really, who could blame them if they decided I wasn't enough? How many alpha men could truly share just one woman?

Chapter 24

Izzy

I was sore, wet, and incredibly *sticky*. I wasn't really sure what else but confused was a good start.

I laid naked and used up between the two men I never thought would want me. Full to the brim with their cum.

"Um-" They both rolled to face me "-I think we should maybe discuss this?" I gestured between us. I needed to make sure that they really wanted to try some sort of *relationship*, that they weren't already planning their escape.

My phone began to buzz from Oliver's table.

"Also, why do you have my phone?"

Oliver rolled over, scooping it up and ignoring my question entirely. "It's the gremlin. She can wait." He silenced it.

"There's not much to talk about, baby girl." Maddox took me by the waist and pulled my back flush to his chest. His noticeably hard erection dug into my ass, and I hissed.

I wiggled in his arms trying to escape.

"You're about to start something you can't finish," Maddox warned me. He was right, my vagina and ass were thoroughly sore. "The answer you're looking for though? You're ours."

I went to argue, but Oliver rolled back and covered my mouth with his hand. "Just listen. I love your quips, but you need to hear this. We want you. Together. The same as we told you last night. Nothing has changed, if anything, we need you even more. We can figure out the rest as we go. I have always ached for you, but you were too young. I intended to let you figure yourself out before you fell into my embrace. Then Maddox came along." Oliver gave said man a mocking glare over my shoulder. "He refused to leave your side, and seriously? You're trouble. I need all the help I can get."

My heart warmed but thinking back to everything he admitted to the night prior, I also felt a bit alarmed. This was a. *Lot*. Their interest, their plan, their *obsession.*

It was bordering on the line of stalkerish, but for some reason it didn't worry me too much. It made me feel *flattered*.

Maybe I should really look into therapy.

I always thought these two were attractive, but now that they showed their interest? I was suddenly shy and didn't know what to say. Plus, the man from last night? That was another problem.

On cue, my phone began to buzz again.

I snatched it from Oliver's hand as he went to silence it and maneuvered out of their grips. "I will be right outside. I promise, but first I need to get clean." As they both went to move, I firmly added, "Alone. Please? I won't be far."

I stepped into the bathroom first. Relieving myself and taking a quick shower. I ignored the dull ache between my legs. I stepped out, drying off, and threw on Oliver's shirt and Maddox's boxers before moving back to the bedroom. Both mens' gazes were directly on my form, following my every move.

"You have two minutes," Maddox stated firmly.

My phone began to ring again. I held up my hand, I didn't want the men to hear me from my adjoining room so instead, I exited into the hallway, answering the phone.

"Hey, mamacita!" I greeted Yara as I took a few steps down the hall.

"Where are you?" Concern dripped from her tone.

"What's wrong?" Yara never was this serious.

"Where are you?" she repeated.

"I'm with Maddox and Oliver. What's going on? You're starting to scare me."

Yara breathed heavily through the phone, obviously relieved. "I'm so sorry, I didn't know. I had my go to guy check him out, but then I just had this *feeling*, and I wish I acted sooner."

My hair turned to pinpoints up and down my arms and legs. Down the hall a door shut. "Yara, you're scaring me."

"Izzy, you need to leave that hotel. Tell Oliver and Maddox. That man from last night wasn't who he said he was. You know him! He was in the reunion photos! Leave now. Go home, get away!"

I didn't realize I was no longer alone, until my phone was yanked from me. I went to scream but a hand holding a scratchy material covered my mouth. The chemical smell was overwhelming.

"Now hush, Miss Kane, it's time for us to be reacquainted."

I met the man's dark eyes before the world spun and darkened around me.

Chapter 25

Oliver

His Isobel

Oliver was finally content. She wasn't running from them like he thought she might. Their archaic plan had worked.

Oliver sat up from the bed. "Go get her, she's taking too long." His phone began to ring and he tugged on his boxers as he walked to the other bed's table and retrieved it.

Why was Yara calling him?

He answered.

"You can kill me later. But Izzy's in trouble. We were talking, but then I heard noises and the phone disconnected."

Oliver's face hardened; he would be killing this girl. Or he would outsource it to Milo. He took long strides to their door, already knowing he wouldn't like what he found on the other side.

"She's not here." Maddox was halfway down the hallway and was walking briskly to the room Isobel was in earlier.

"Speak," Oliver demanded of the woman on the phone.

"I fucked up." Yara quickly explained to Oliver what happened.

How the man that touched his Isobel *knew* her.

"Something isn't right! My security team has never failed before, I even ran it past Emil. There's more to this."

Oliver swore, but he had no more time to deal with this nuisance. "We will find her, but you better hope it's in time. She is mine. Nobody else is allowed to have her."

"I fucking knew it. You obsessive freak! You're no good for her either!" Yara screamed out as he disconnected the call.

She wasn't wrong, but frankly? He didn't give a single fuck.

He typed in a number and called their go-to. He was a jack of all trades and though he had never met him in person, Oliver trusted him to protect Izzy more than he cared to admit.

Milo was never too far away when needed.

"Sir?"

"We have a situation." Oliver shortly recapped what was going on.

That there was someone at the reunion after her. That she had most likely been taken. They needed the location of the camera feeds and how long she had been missing.

Milo stayed silent until the end. "I understand. I will provide updates when available."

Chapter 26

Izzy

I tried to unstick my eyes as I slowly came to. Pain throbbed against my temple. I attempted to move, but I found myself bound. I blinked a few times, but immediately realized something was limiting my sight. I could only make out vague shapes past whatever rested over my face.

I had just a few moments of complete confusion, before memories flashed through my mind. Yara's phone call. The mystery man. His black desolate eyes.

"Sebastian?" I called out.

"Oh, so now we are on a first name basis, dear Bel?" Smooth, clammy fingers stroked my hand and I did my best to contain my disgust.

I remained silent.

"We're back where both of our lives changed forever. Who knew that you would be another stupid, stupid girl." He ripped off the material covering my eyes and I found us back on our school's roof. The full moon shone brightly over us as I examined Sebastian. He looked positively unhinged. Eyes widened, hair in disarray, a dark stain covering his white shirt. Mouth opened showing sharpened teeth that glinted in the moonlight.

How did my stupid self ever think this man was anything but evil? Oh that's right, I was a teenager that he preyed on.

"Wearing another man's clothes. Covered in cum. You were always a whore. But that's why we ended up like this, isn't it?" A knife suddenly appeared in Sebastian's hand glinting before swiping downwards, slicing my shirt in half.

The material fell open, baring my chest to the disgusting predator. A thin line of blood dripped down from where he nicked my skin. The pain was a stark reminder of the monster that stood before me.

His lips curled cruelly.

I was going to be okay. Oliver and Maddox were going to find me. This was just a bad nightmare. When in doubt, bullshit my way out. Except neither of them knew about Sebastian. Only one other person did. The one that saved me all those years ago. When I was a stupid naïve girl.

It was my senior year of high school. Oliver was once more overseas and Yara had her first ever boyfriend. I felt exceptionally alone and I was being targeted by bullies. Frequently.

I was sitting anxiously in my calculus class when it finally hit a breaking point. The rest of the class left, but I stayed behind, staring at an empty wall. Wishing desperately for an escape. For a light to shine through.

"Are you alright, Miss Kane?"

The honeyed voice dragged me from my thoughts and I met our teacher's concerned eyes. "Sorry, Mr. York. It's just been difficult, I feel lonely." I offered up a sheepish smile. I knew high school wasn't the place for people like me.

At the time I didn't notice the glint in his eye, the way the word lonely *brought forth the demon that hid beneath his skin. "Oh, Miss Kane, I un-*

derstand. I am very much an oddity both here and in my day-to-day life. I'm heading to the coffee shop right outside of school, let me buy you a coffee?"

I started to protest.

"It's fine, I do this for all of my students when they need extra help in their studies. It's where we meet for tutoring." He placed a reassuring hand on my shoulder. I learned later it was all a lie. He was just trying to make me feel more comfortable. Easier to manipulate.

It worked.

It went on and on like that for quite some time, until the coffee turned into gifts. His hand on my shoulder that day gradually drifted downward to my thighs as the time progressed. He did it slowly, but even still, I began to realize there wasn't something quite right with his attention. I was ashamed to admit it, though, because it would show how useless I was without Yara and Oliver.

It hit a boiling point when he walked me up to the roof. He wanted to show me the view as the sun was beginning to set. I should have known better. He kissed me. He played it off as an accident.

"I think we should stop this. I appreciate your company, but I need to focus on myself. On graduating and college." I backed away slowly until I reached the door. Reaching behind me to open it. It wouldn't budge. The terror I had been keeping at bay began to consume me.

"Now, now, now." It was the first time I truly saw Sebastian York for what he was. A demon. "You are not leaving here without letting me have a taste. I have been patient with you, but it's time. You need to let this happen."

He attacked before I could move, ripping me from the door and pushing me onto the ground. I did my best to scream, but he quickly covered my mouth so hardly any sound could escape. He was much larger and stronger than I was. I hadn't learned self-defense; I didn't know what to do.

I found myself giving up. I numbed myself to his cold fingers as they pried my clothes from my stiff body. I let the tears fall as I heard him unzip his pants. I was fully naked when the door to the roof slammed open.

I didn't expect my nerdy quiet classmate Emilio to be there, I most definitely didn't expect him to be holding a gun.

"Get the fuck off of her!"

I couldn't believe I ever thought this a nice man, he dripped poison in everything that he did. He did whisper such sweet lies, but it didn't matter. I should have known better.

If not for Emilio, I would never have escaped Sebastian's clutches. Emilio and I were inseparable after that.

And that horrible day on the roof was the last I had seen of Sebastian.

Until the reunion.

Chapter 27

Sebastian York

Bel was his. She always had been, but then that *fucker* had shot him. Left him on this very roof to die, but he was resilient. He was an insistent and unrelenting man. And now his tenacity had finally paid off, she was in his possession again.

When he finally found that she was living in New York, he booked a one-way plane ticket only to be disappointed by her constant supervision. Why did she have not one, not two, but three bodyguards? They made it impossible for him to infiltrate her life.

So, he waited. Bided his time. When he found she had booked a ticket here, he knew she would be attending the reunion. He had to play it safe. He didn't want anyone to suspect his intent.

Seeing her again? Fuck, it had done more to him than he cared to admit. Typically, he lost interest as a woman aged, and Bel was pushing thirty. But there was something about her sweet, innocent, round face. Her sweet, soft voice. He couldn't quite pinpoint what it was, but it had him chomping at the bit to get her where he wanted her.

Underneath him.

When she disappeared from the reunion, he tried to find her but lost her on the road. No matter, he wasn't a quitter and he had finally gotten lucky. Driving along the congregation of hotels, he spotted Yara getting into a rideshare. He knew Bel would never be too far from her precious friend.

Sebastian was well acquainted with this town. Enough so that when he went into the hotel, the receptionist knew better than to tell him no when he asked for her room number. He booked the room across from hers. He broke into Bel's first, but she wasn't there. No problem, it was just a matter of patience.

He took up watch in his room and a few hours later, he witnessed a mongrel manhandling her into a different room. Shortly after, another entered the same room. The one right next to hers. Sebastian was enraged.

How dare she touch them?

It took everything in him not to bust down the door and take her from the men, except he knew that wouldn't end well.

He never moved from his post, and he couldn't believe it when they let her step into the hallway. Alone.

And now here she was, in his clutches. His dick strained at his pants attempting to escape and find its home.

Her sweet little kitty would be his.

Except she wasn't paying him any attention. Sebastian slapped the girl's face.

"Fucking look at me!" he roared into the air.

Bel gave Sebastian her full attention. His anger subsided, but only just a bit. He had so many things planned to catch up with his Bel.

He shifted his gaze as a reflective glare caught in his periphery.

The full moon's light illuminated something metallic in a window from the building across from theirs. He realized what it was just in time for half of his face to implode. Blood spewing everywhere while simultaneously a loud noise rang out.

Chapter 28

Milo

His Bella Isa

Target neutralized. Three for three. This trip turned out to be much more fulfilling than Milo expected. It was finally time for her to come back to him.

He had drugged Yara so she couldn't come to the reunion. He didn't want her to recognize him. He could tell she almost had when he gave her the food, but thankfully his disguise had worked well enough.

Unfortunately, he forgot how documented reunions were. He couldn't believe his carelessness. Yara had seen a picture of him there. It could have upended his plans.

He needed to be more careful.

He had watched Isa from the shadows for years, keeping her safe, waiting for her to be ready to return to him.

He had fulfilled her darkest desires. Fucking her senseless, waking her up on his fingers.

He had returned to her tonight, just as he promised.

Milo packed up the sniper rifle, sent a message to one of his family member's to secure it and another message to clean up the mess that was now Sebastian York. He walked briskly down the stairs and then across the lawn to the school, opening the door and heading up to the school's roof.

He didn't realize he was sprinting until he was halfway up the stairs.

It was time.

Slowing for just a moment, he called Oliver. "I have located Isa. She is safe. I will bring her to you both. ETA two hours." He ignored Oliver's rage and demand for his location by simply disconnecting the call.

Those were two problems he would need to deal with soon and carefully. He knew how attached his Isa was to the two unworthy men.

How obsessed they were with her. It was why he wormed his way onto their security team. Why he made himself invaluable. The men never even bothered to meet him in person. Instead, they just sent Milo to do their dirty work.

Milo slowly took the last few steps to the roof, thinking through exactly how to go about this, but then again, it was Isa; she would understand.

Pushing the door open, he paid the trash that was Sebastian's body no attention.

His caramel eyes found her beautiful ones. They were glassy and dripping with tears. He stepped quickly to her. He stamped down the rage that mixed with lust at the sight of her blouse cut open. Of her full breasts laid bare.

"You were at the reunion?" Isa gasped out.

He quickly untied her. "I was," Milo confirmed. He wrenched his shirt off and gently tugged it over her head.

"Why do I feel like we know each other?" Isa interrogated him.

Even in the middle of a traumatic experience, she was the firecracker he remembered her to be. He scooped her easily into his arms and carried her bridal-style off of the godforsaken roof.

He thought he'd killed Sebastian the first time around, but all he did was make him go into hiding.

"Well, that's easy. You do know me, my Bella Isa."

Isa gasped again and tried to extricate herself from his grip. He was almost to the bottom of the stairs now and walked brusquely to the back of an SUV. One of his men held the door open for him.

"It's okay. Stay still, I've got you." Milo didn't blame her for not recognizing him. When they first met, he hadn't been more than a gangly nerdy teenager, but he grew up. He dedicated himself to two things. Isa and his family.

"Emilio?" she whispered out. His Bella Isa could call him whatever she wanted and he would always answer.

He smiled into her hair, kissing it. The Wall, Milo, Emil. He had gone by many names over the years, but in high school it was simply Emilio.

Emilio tucked the precious woman into the vehicle before settling down beside her. He vowed then and there to never let her go again. "That's right. Such a good girl."

Ten years prior

His Bella Isa

Emilio was tired of this school. Exhausted from the day-to-day monotony. He was ready to drop out and he would have years ago. If it weren't for her.

Isobel. His Bella Isa. Well, she wasn't exactly his, but he dreamed that one day she would be. Except in his family's line of work, he was afraid to ever bring her into the fold.

Instead, he tried his best to keep her safe from the shadows. She was being relentlessly bullied, but he could fix that. James finally let her be after he took matters into his own hands. After he beat the shit out of the sniveling teenager.

If James ever spoke to her again though? He wouldn't be walking away from the encounter.

Emilio thought that was all he needed to do to keep her safe.

But recently?

Something wasn't quite right.

Emilio had been around numerous soulless men; it didn't take him long to pinpoint his feelings of unease. Isa was spending more and more time around her teacher, Sebastian York. He seemed happy, jovial, good. Too good. The man was a rose covered in sharp thorns. Every creature in the wild that was purposefully bright and colorful was venomous. Sebastian was no different and Emilio knew it was only a matter of time before the teacher crossed a line.

Emilio was just finishing up a job for his family when he checked Isa's location and anxiety sunk into his gut. She was still at school. This late?

He cursed and ordered his driver to make a U-turn. Emilio knew he should have dealt with this problem sooner.

Upon arriving, Emilio heard it. Isa's quiet muffled scream coming from the roof. He wasted no time; he grabbed his gun and ran up the stairs.

Throwing open the roof's door he saw the disgusting man attacking her.

"Get the fuck off of her!" he yelled at the predator.

The man's dick was only inches from touching Emilio's precious Isa when he stopped. Emilio was on the predator before he realized what he was doing and pistol whipped him across the face. His driver had joined them at this point and pressed the barrel of his gun to the predator's head.

With the situation under control, Emilio examined Isa. He did his best to avert his eyes from her naked form. He found that her face was wet and the tears that streamed down her face, he wished to lick away.

He shook his head, clearing the thought. Later. He needed to help her now. To make sure she would be okay from this.

He might be a killer by default, but he would never attack an innocent. Never assault a girl.

Scalding anger shot through his veins as he shrugged out of his baggy leather jacket and handed it to her. He found her pants and helped her into them as she shrugged into the jacket. She was shivering but also giving him a hard look.

"Why do you have a gun?" she questioned.

"Later." He turned to his driver. "Take her to the car. Take her to my home, make sure she's comfortable."

Isa protested, "If you think I am going to a second undisclosed location after THAT, you are out of your goddamn mind."

Emilio pointed his gun at the teacher and gestured for his driver to hand his gun over. "Take this." He handed it to her. He aligned her fingers where they needed to be. "This is the safety and when it's off you just pull the trigger. If you aim, you must be willing to shoot."

Isa stiffened her shoulders and snatched the gun from him, she immediately pointed the gun in the teacher's direction, flicked the safety, and shot into the ground, inches from the man's dick. Sebastian attempted to jerk away, but Emilio stepped forward holding him in place.

"Okay," she agreed. She spared one last glance back before following his driver away.

"You don't know what you're doing," Sebastian threatened.

Emilio didn't bother arguing. His mind was made up the moment he saw the man on top of the struggling Isa. He waited until she was far enough away to not hear the noise before he shot the man in the chest.

He called his clean-up crew. "Party of one. No trace." He left the roof without a backwards glance.

That was the last he saw of Sebastian but later learned when the clean-up crew arrived, 20 minutes after he left to go after his Isa, the only evidence of the predator was a puddle of blood.

After that, Emilio waited until his targets stopped breathing. He never let another man survive his judgment.

Especially not when it came to his precious Bella Isa.

Come to Head

A Dark Why Choose Romance

Sage RelleAnne

Rainbow Publishing House LLC

Proofread by Anna Lisa Vitale and Ashleigh Voros of Split Leaf Saturdays book editing

First edition 2024.

Introduction

Hi all,

This has gone through several rounds of editing, including proofreading, but if you still find mistakes, please let me know! My email is: sagerelleanne@gmail.com

As a reminder: I write in both first and third person. This will be pretty consistent among all of my novels. For this one Izzy is in first POV and the men will be in third. Most have loved this, but some have not.

This book is part of my Darkest Desires world. You MUST read Come to Bed first as it is the first part of Izzy's story.

Now that, that's out of the way, thank you so very kindly for giving my book a read. I greatly appreciate your support!

Okay I promise that's everything (besides the triggers).

VERY IMPORTANT

This book has quite a few trigger warnings.

For an extensive in-depth list please reach out to me at: sagerelleanne@gmail.com

Brief outline of triggers:

There is a TW that is a spoiler, **but if you need an extensive list**, please let me know via email and I will send it to you.

Brutål & graphic un@living

Somno & dorma

Dub con & CNC

Kidnapping & t0rtúre

Stãlkers

Loss of loved ones

Mention of SA (not on page or graphic or to fmc)

N,

I dove headfirst into writing this book on the day I found out you were going to die.

(This is the sequel to the one you told your husband not to read).

I'm going to be honest; it was hard to give it a happy ending.

But we all deserve our happiness.

Your support in all my endeavors was and will always be appreciated.

Love you always.

May you end up exactly where you wish to be.

-Your favorite (only) niece

Sage

PS. I feel like you would love that this is printed over a woman's bare ass.

This one is for all you that use humor to cope.

That joke away your tears.

That laugh through your grief.

That accept the insanity of life and still keep on trucking.

May you find your ~~crystal ashtray~~ peace.

som·no·phil·i·a

A paraphilia characterized by sexual arousal or interest in engaging in sexual activities with someone that is asleep or unconscious.

Prologue

Emilio did his best to quietly creep into the room, for he knew his precious Isa slept soundly inside. Just as he knew that when she awoke, it would be to him. Inside her. Filling her up, fucking her, and fulfilling her darkest desire. *Again*. He might just have to fight off two men in the process.

Chapter 1

Izzy

Over Ten Years Ago

Shock. Denial. *Anger.*

I shot at a man. I was almost raped. By my teacher.

Emilio Castillo saved me? With a *gun*? What the fuck?

And now I was shoved into a room lined in velvet and darkened tones in what was essentially a mansion. On the second floor. Waiting for him.

Why am I not leaving?

I was a fucking idiot. That was the only excuse I had. I clutched the gun tighter to my chest; the safety was still off.

I heard the front door open and close downstairs, followed by footsteps.

I tensed, squaring my shoulders, unsure of what to expect.

Emilio burst into the room, searching for me. The shock from the door banging open caused me to squeeze. The gun went off, shooting into the wall to our left.

"Fuck Isa! Gun safety is important. Put the goddamn safety back on." Emilio wasn't an intimidating guy; he was a senior just like me. He was tall but lanky, and my guess was that I weighed more than he did. But his white shirt was sprayed with what was discernibly fresh blood.

"What happened?" I did my best to not let my voice break. "Isa? Do we know each other?" He looked vaguely familiar but not well enough for him to have a nickname for me.

Emilio followed my attention to his shirt, looking down, and his face shuttered. "An altercation, but everything is okay." He completely ignored my last question as he pulled the same gun I had seen him holding before from behind him, gently setting it down on his dresser. "Are you okay?"

I wasn't.

That one question deflated the last of my reserves. I put the safety back as he had shown me and set my gun down gently, mirroring him. As soon as it was out of my grip, Emilio surged forward and hauled me into his warm embrace.

He began stroking my back, and I became overtly aware that all I wore was his half-zipped jacket and a pair of leggings.

I was self-conscious. I was distraught.

I felt.

Raw.

A thousand painful prickles of what-ifs littered up and down my skin as I allowed myself to find solace in Emilio's embrace.

"He tried to—" I couldn't say it aloud. Speak it into existence. It would make it real. It would make me face the countless decisions I made that allowed that to happen to me.

"I know." Emilio swept my hair back and wiped away the tears I didn't realize were steadily pouring. He cupped my cheeks in his large hands. "I can see it in your face, but Isa? None of that was your fault. That man was—*is*—a predator."

I stared up into Emilio's caramel eyes and lost myself in the softness that swirled in their depths. There was evidence he wasn't a good man, that even though he was my age, he had seen and done more than I hoped to ever, but I needed comfort. I needed something to fill me. Anything besides this pain. I almost lost my virginity to a horrible man.

Who better to give it to than a practical stranger?

Why not take back my control? I'm going to remember this night anyway, I might as well rewrite it the best I can.

Trauma did strange things to people.

"Fuck me," I rasped out, staring unblinkingly up at him.

Emilio stiffened. "Isa, you don't owe me anything. You don't need to prove something. You just went through a horrible event and aren't thinking clearly."

Once more, self-consciousness gnashed its sharp teeth into my gut.

Other people's words ricocheted in my head.

I had too many curves. I wasn't a typical beauty. No one would ever love me.

I redirected my gaze to the room—the opulent space, the dark velvet colors, the two guns on the dresser, a window with the blinds pulled shut. I was on the second floor, but maybe I could make my escape through it?

Emilio squeezed my face with his large, sturdy hands, the pads of his thumbs stroking my cheeks gently. "Stop whatever is going through that beautiful mind of yours. I want you more than anything. But you just went through something traumatic, and I don't want to take advantage of you."

Those were the words he said, but I felt his length stiffen against my belly, pressing into me.

His arousal ignited my own.

"Please?" With renewed confidence and just the right amount of bravery, I raised onto my tiptoes, stretching up and yanking him down.

I could tell I had shocked him, that he hadn't expected it.

It was the only reason my move worked.

I smashed my lips to his.

He tasted metallic. Bitter. With a harsh bite.

I love it.

He was still for a moment, but then his soft lips moved against mine. His hands exploring.

One found my hair, tangling into it, pulling me closer.

The other to my ass, gripping it tightly, causing sparks of electricity to shoot directly to the heat furling in my belly.

I dove further into him, willing him to take away the pain that still flooded me, the uneasiness that wound so tight in my heart I could barely breathe. In this moment, I delivered everything I felt into the kiss, and he accepted it. He allowed me to seize control, to create this moment the way I needed to, to alter my first kiss.

If anyone asked? This would be it. My first sexual encounter.

He would be the permanent marker I used to black out Sebastian York.

The desire and pleasure I felt, the warmth of his hands as he held me to him, the way he let me dominate.

The odd feeling that this was where I belonged, the passion that engulfed my heart, the inferno threatening to light me on fire.

Emilio didn't push back; he just allowed me to take. And take. *And take.* Our tongues danced an entire song before I separated breathlessly.

"Please?" I begged again.

Darkness shrouded Emilio's face, but he jerked his head in a nod. "Yes, but I can't promise you anything. My world isn't safe for you."

My attention again found the two guns, a testament to his warning. However, we were graduating in two weeks, and after the summer, I was determined to move away. This incident solidified that.

"Until the end of summer?" I asked, watching him carefully.

Unmistakable agony etched across Emilio's face, his lips curving downwards into a frown, his forehead creasing, a wrinkle forming between his brow, but he nodded his agreement.

He untangled himself from me, stepping back, and his frown twisted to a confident smile. His hypnotizing eyes held mine while he shed his clothes. In a flash of motion, he ripped his crimson-stained white T-shirt off. While he was lanky and his face hadn't lost all of its youth, it was easy to tell that he was unmistakably muscular. Especially shirtless. My hand advanced on its own accord, tracing the tattoo over his heart.

A burgundy moth.

His bulky hand covered mine, rough digits stroking my skin. "My sister's favorite animal." He cracked a slight wistful grin before dropping his grip on my hand, leaving a trail of tingles in its wake.

Before I could blink, he moved back and tore off his remaining clothes, completely distracting me from his tattoo.

His impressive cock bobbed up towards his stomach on full display and stole my attention.

Is this even a good idea?

I gulped, suddenly unsure, before moving my gaze upwards. Studying him.

There was clear, unmistakable interest—key in on his hard cock—even still, he wasn't pushing me. He wasn't trying to take anything from me. He was just observing me with a soft expression and a lopsided grin.

I expected to feel uneasy at the attention. At the similarity to Sebastian's attention.

Except, Emilio wasn't watching me as Sebastian had. When Sebastian was on top of me, I finally noticed what I had ignored before. The evil glint, the predatorial behavior, the manipulation. The signs had always been there, I'd just ignored them.

I felt in my gut that being with Emilio would be a safe encounter, but could I even trust that?

"We can stop, Isa. You don't have to do this." He shifted, picking up his clothes to put back on, and it pierced through my nerves.

Emilio *wouldn't* hurt me. This was *my choice.*

"I do." *Have a choice.*

He chuckled softly, dropping his shirt back to the ground and cocking an eyebrow.

I want to do this.

I needed to wipe away the memories of Seb—

My line of thought was cut off as Emilio moved back into my space.

"Then it's your turn, my Bella Isa."

There he went with that nickname.

He gently, *gradually* reached up, unzipping the borrowed jacket and letting it fall to the ground, allowing me plenty of time to shove him away.

I didn't.

With the clothing discarded, my breasts were freed; the weight of which instantly pulled at my back.

I went to wrap my arms around my chest to cover the stretch marks painted there, but Emilio tapped them gently.

"I am going to fuck you, Isa, but first, you're going to let me see you."

"I—"

"We all have our imperfections sweet Isa, but what is an imperfection to some," he paused to yank down my leggings, "is stunning beauty to another."

I struggled a bit against my own self-consciousness, my cheeks flushing, embarrassment coursing through my veins.

"You are so beautiful. You would bring nations to their knees. Please never hide yourself from me. I want to see everything there is of you. Anything you are willing to offer. You are *my* Bella Isa."

My face heated at his compliment. It felt sincere. I hadn't received too many of those over the years—besides from Yara.

He pressed lightly against me, forcing me to step back until the backs of my knees hit the bed. Gently, he laid me back on it, my legs still firmly planted on the ground.

"Just like that, let me see you. Touch you. *Taste you*. And if you need me to stop, just tell me and I will."

His words washed warmly across me.

In this room, with this man, there was no space for insecurity. Instead, I shut my eyes and allowed myself to fall into this moment.

Sturdy hands found my thighs, spreading my legs apart.

"Just like that, relax for me, Isa." Rough fingers skirted along the apex of my thighs. "Guide me."

With my eyes still closed, I extended my hand, placing one of his over my clit. I had never been touched by another person before like this, but I knew what I liked doing to myself.

"Please," I murmured.

That was all he needed to start.

He began to work circles on the spot. At first, it didn't feel good. It was too dry, and I voiced that to him. My skin heated at the awkwardness, but then he moved to my entrance stealing some of the wetness there before returning to my clit. He didn't seem overly experienced, but his willingness to listen and do as I asked was making up for that.

"Like that," I moaned out, arching off of the bed as he rubbed it.

He grunted. "Good, keep telling me what you like. What you want."

I hummed my agreement.

"And then..." He slowly pushed a finger into me, just one.

The sudden intrusion was too much at first, and it startled me, but then I found myself bucking onto it. Wanting more.

"Curl it," I commanded.

He chuckled, a deep, heady baritone, but did as I requested.

Pressing into a spot that I had used my own fingers on before. But with his? The feeling was ten-fold.

How could I go back to a stagnant level of pleasure after this? He was taking me higher than I had been before.

"You look fucking beautiful like this. Let me play with you a bit longer. I want to try something else too." He removed the hand on my clit, and I wanted to protest, but then his wet hot mouth replaced it. Licking, biting, sucking.

He added another finger, and it slid easier than the first.

"Fuck!" I exhaled, my hands digging into the sheets below as I undulated up into him.

He was speedwalking me to a point that I had only been with my vibrators.

"Mmmm." The noise from him was muffled as he continued his ministrations.

The pleasure made it hard to guide him now, but he didn't need it, he was using my body to tell him what I needed. Every time I made a particularly loud moan, he would pull back, frustrating me again and again.

Eventually, after he brought me to the edge with his fingers and mouth for a third time, he removed them and lifted my legs over his shoulders.

I heard the sound of plastic tearing.

My eyes shot open to find him staring at me as he slid a condom into place. My face heated at his attention. I knew it would hurt, but even still,

I was going to go through with this. I was more than halfway into the ride; I wouldn't turn back now. I couldn't.

"Are you ready?" His soulful eyes sparked something profound inside me, and I was already regretting our agreement to separate. This man was an addiction I never wanted to kick.

"Fuck, please." I was a needy mess; he had muddled my mind, electrified my body, and lit fire to my nerves. In the beginning, it had been awkward and uncomfortable, evidence that he wasn't overly experienced. He hadn't touched me the way that I wanted him to. But he had quickly picked up on my cues and followed my guidance. His willingness to learn was almost as addicting as his touch.

Why didn't he find me first instead of Mr. York?

That thought was knocked firmly from my mind as he slowly began to push into my body, stretching me. I hissed past the searing pain, and he pitched forward, placing butterfly kisses across my face and neck.

"You are doing so well, just a bit more." He reached down, rubbing my clit softly, and the stimulation allowed him to sink the rest of the way into my body.

I moaned out and began to enjoy riding the cusp of pain and pleasure.

Emilio rolled his hips softly and gently into me, and I could feel his adoration as he pulled me taut.

He kept the same soothing rhythm for a bit longer before he was satisfied I could handle more.

He bent over me. "Just a bit harder, you can take it, " he whispered into my ear, nibbling it.

The moving of his hips turned to hard snaps, and the tension that had already built boiled over; with one last pinch to my clit, I came with a whimper.

A few more thrusts, and he stilled as he filled me.

When he slowly pulled out from me, I immediately missed the feeling of him.

At the sight of blood, he shuddered. "Did I go too hard?" His eyes searched mine.

I shook my head. "I was a virgin," I murmured, suddenly embarrassed again.

Emilio's face did a one-eighty, turning as bright as it could, the dark confidence vanishing. "Me too."

His words didn't fully sink in until he returned, tugging me up.

"Let's shower, the hot water should help the soreness."

I let him lead me to it as his words sloshed around in my head. "You were a virgin, and you let some random girl take it?"

Emilio stepped into the shower, wrenching me in before turning his full attention to me. "You are not some random girl. You are everything that I have ever wanted, and I will spend the next few months showing you what it means to be loved by a guy like me. I will show you what you deserve. All I ask is that you never accept anything less."

Emilio kept his promise until the end of summer, and I felt more loved than I thought possible. But I didn't keep my promise. I continued to make horrible choices, always chasing the high of the man that I first gave myself to—body, heart, and soul.

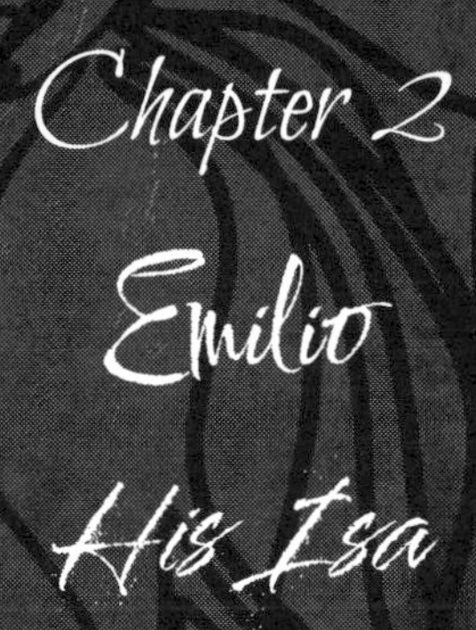

Chapter 2
Emilio
His Isa

Exactly Ten Years Ago

Emilio watched his Isa sleep for the last time. She would be leaving for New York with Oliver tomorrow, and he would be stuck here. Forced to continue his family's legacy. Forced to be the head of his family.

He absentmindedly rubbed the tattoo on his bare chest. He couldn't save his sister from this life, but he would not let the same fate befall this precious woman. Emilio stroked Isa affectionately as she breathed heavily in her sleep.

A noise startled him from his contemplations. He extended, gripping his gun under the mattress as the door to his bedroom was silently nudged open.

He loosened his hold on the weapon when he saw who it was.

"Kazi. You're here." He acknowledged the man, unwrapping himself from Izzy.

He crept off the bed, scrutinizing the man who stood in the doorway. Kazi was clearly aggrieved, hands clenched into fists, shoulder squared, lips flattened into a line.

"Sir," the newcomer clipped out.

It was almost comical hearing older men call Emilio sir, but he was used to it by now.

His sister's death, followed immediately by his father's death six years ago, had caused a shift in power, and he had been forced to grow up quickly.

Too quickly.

"You have your orders?" Emilio questioned, his attention flickering to Isa to ensure she still slept soundly.

Kazi was newer to their fold, but Emilio trusted him.

He had shown promise, and Emilio needed the right person for this...job.

Kazi took a moment too long to respond, and Emilio stepped further from the bed into the man's face.

Looking down at him, he examined Kazi's expressions critically.

Kazi heaved a sigh, relaxing out of his tense posture. "I just don't want to move to California, but I guess if it's only temporarily."

Emilio smirked caustically; he didn't have the heart to tell Kazi this would be his permanent assignment.

Emilio might be letting Isa leave his side and move away, but that didn't mean he didn't plan on keeping tabs on every piece of her life. And Kazi's job? Well, that would be to watch over her best friend, Yara.

Isa cared about Yara more than almost anything else in the world and that meant Emilio needed to ensure Yara's safety, if only to keep his Bella happy. He didn't trust the precocious Yara to stay out of trouble and that was where Kazi came into play.

Isa shifted behind him.

"Go, " he ordered, shoving Kazi back and shutting the door.

"Emilio?" Izzy's husky, sleep-ladened voice swept across the room to him.

"Coming, Bella. Are you ready for another round?"

He walked carefully back to the bed, finding her bright eyes in the otherwise darkened room.

Fuck, she was a sight. Her bare chest was on display, hickeys adorning her alabaster skin. His marks. "Soon enough, I'm going to wake you up on my dick, or would you prefer to wake up on my fingers?"

"Fingers," Izzy laughed lyrically, but he watched as she subconsciously rubbed her thighs together.

He wasn't joking.

"Can you..." Her voice turned unsure, putting him on edge.

"Can I, what?"

She was sitting up in his bed now, and he moved his rough fingers, skating along her soft lips.

"Can you just hold me, please? I'm scared. What if I fail?" Isa whispered the words against his skin.

He immediately shifted, wrapping her in his arms.

True to form they had spent as much time as they could together in the past several months, but tomorrow she would be leaving for New York to start up her business with Oliver.

Oliver had been home for a few days at the end of their summer together. Emilio was afraid she would run back to him, but instead she came up with the idea to leave altogether. At her request, Oliver had immediately left for New York with the promise Isa would follow him in a week.

Oliver. Oliver. Oliver.

Emilio was tired of hearing the other man's name and knew Oliver wasn't the nice selfless man Isa claimed him to be.

He already had plans to infiltrate her life, even as they lived so far apart, but he didn't voice that.

"You are going to succeed." He stroked her back, tugging her to him tightly.

Her face found the crook of his neck, and she burrowed there.

He felt the tears as she began to cry, but he didn't mention them. Instead, he continued to hold her, rubbing gentle circles on her back.

After a bit, she pulled back from him, her glistening eyes the only evidence of her distress.

"Emilio, this doesn't change anything, but I need you to know."

Emilio reached up wiping her tears away with the pads of his thumbs, keeping his attention on her the entire time. "What is it, Bella?"

"I... This started as using you. As a way to escape the pain of what almost happened."

Physically Emilio attempted not to react. But internally? A fire pilfered across his skin, darkening his vision, pounding into his heart, infiltrating every part of him. Molten rage. Emilio stamped down the anger that threatened to crawl up his throat. It wasn't directed towards Isa.

The pedophile.

He had shot Sebastian. Sebastian should have died, but he hadn't. Instead, he was gone by the time his *family's* clean-up crew arrived to clear the body.

Sebastian hadn't been found since. It was Emilio's main regret. It was his excuse to never let Isa out of his sight.

Isa paused, unsure of his silence.

"Go on," he pressed gently, dipping forward to pepper her face in soft kisses soothing his own soul with each brush against her skin.

"I know I'm too young, and I probably don't know any better, but Emilio, I do—" An unexpected hiccup cut her off, and her cheeks turned pink. The hiccups hit her hard and she puffed her face as she held her breath aggressively.

No matter how adorable she looked, Emilio knew better than to laugh right now.

She let the air whoosh out and waited just a moment before shutting her eyes and squeezing them. "Fuck. I love you, dammit!"

Emilio dropped his hold on her in shock.

No. That wasn't—

No. Emilio didn't deserve—

No. Isa couldn't—

His brain short-circuited as all his plans swirled in his mind.

In every scenario, he hadn't accounted for her to actually *care* about him. To *love* him.

"But don't get the wrong impression. I'm not breaking our promise." Her eyes were open now, and they were boring into him.

He snapped out of his stupor. His brain switched gears.

He wouldn't keep an innocent woman tethered to him.

But if she loved him? If she was willing to? What if she returned to him on her own accord?

Maybe this didn't have to be good-bye. Maybe he could get what he wanted most. Maybe she could be *his*.

The spiraling questions and maybes piled up as an unhinged plan formed.

"Isa. I want to make a new promise. A pact."

"What is it?"

He jumped on her, forcing Isa flat to the bed, his hands landing on the mattress on each side of her head, his lips centimeters from hers.

She let out a cute squeak of surprise. Her hair was a disheveled mess, her eyes coated in sleep, her body marred with bruises.

Perfect. She was absolutely perfect.

"A marriage pact." He pushed his lips to hers for a brief, searing connection. "In 10 years, if we're both single, we get married. To each other."

She spluttered, "What? I—that's silly! That's what kids who don't know any better say! And what about the *danger?*"

Isa didn't even know the beginning of the *danger*, just that it existed. In 10 years, he would tell her. She didn't need to know now, she wasn't ready.

Especially of her own ties to it.

"Well, Isa," Emilio pressed his forehead to hers, his lips curling cruelly, "you said you used me, and now you say you love me. You hurt my feelings, Bella. And what's the harm? In 10 years, I'm sure you will be settled down." Not if he could help it. "And it won't be dangerous for you then. I will make sure of it."

He just needed to kill a few pesky men, find a pedophile, and conquer a town. He could manage that in 10 years.

And even if he couldn't...

He leaned back just a bit. He wouldn't pressure her too much, he would let her decide on her own.

But did she know this was her last chance to escape him?

If she agreed... Well, he would allow her 10 years.

But not a day longer.

Her eyes flickered between his. He could tell she wasn't convinced, but then, to his surprise, she nodded softly. "Okay, Emilio."

He couldn't help the joy that pilfered through him. "I love you too, Bella Isa," he susurrated into her ear before rolling off her.

She reached over, pinching him on the head of his dick. "Nothing is ever easy with you!" she huffed.

He ignored her protests as he hugged her against him. He needed as much of her as he could have. Her fingers on the tip of his dick had only caused it to harden and he grinded it into her luscious ass from behind.

His Isa let out a breathy mewl.

The previous depression was replaced with determination.

Tonight was their last night.

For now.

But in 10 years, he would return, and she wouldn't be settled down.

Emilio would make sure of it.

She would be his wife.

Chapter 3

Izzy

Present Day

My head was throbbing, and nothing made sense. I had dreamed that Emilio would return to my life one day, but not like this.

And who was this man in place of the teenage boy I had given myself to all those years ago?

I hadn't even recognized him at the reunion for fuck's sake.

I wiped away my tears and turned in the seat to him. "Where are you taking me?"

Emilio didn't meet my eyes immediately, reaching behind him instead. "Sign this NDA first, and then I can answer your questions."

I glanced down at the paper as he thrust a pen into my hand. I scanned it cursorily before signing. He took it and replaced it with a similar form.

I signed the form, only for him to replace it with another, and so on, for 10 more pages. The shock of what had just happened with Sebastian was wearing off, and in its place, annoyance grew. "Emilio, what is this?"

"I can't have you in my life without this. It is just precautionary." He leaned forward, pressing his forehead to mine. "You trust me, don't you? You know I would never hurt you? Don't you, my good girl? My Bella?"

Something about his words mixed with his guttural tone sparked a memory to the forefront of my mind.

"You? It was you! You met with Yara? You were the one, you..." My face flushed in embarrassment. I should be angry, but instead, I was *happy*. Relieved that it had been Emilio. That it wasn't some stranger but a man that I was already intrinsically connected to.

"I fulfilled your darkest desires and woke you up on my fingers? Yes Isa. It was me. Now, there's one more thing we have to do before you reunite with the two annoyances that have infiltrated your life."

I fell back into my seat. The leather was sticking to my bare thighs, and I was acutely aware I was fully dressed in other men's clothes.

Maddox's boxers and Emilio's shirt.

Emilio followed my attention, leaning forward to survey me. His eyes darkened as he found the fresh marks left on my body and then stopped on my bottom half. "I suppose this outfit will have to do. I need to get you back to Maddox and Oliver shortly."

My hands fanned my lap, gripping the material uncomfortably and wiping the sweat away. I was doing my best to stay calm, cool, *and collected,* but I was, in fact, not any of those things.

There was a hummingbird in my heart fluttering its wings and a typhoon in my stomach rolling with the vehicle. The only reason I hadn't completely dissolved into a puddle of irreparable mush was that I knew Emilio. I *trusted* him. At least I did at one time.

I didn't bother to ask how he seemed to know Maddox and Oliver. "Where are we going?" I chose the most pressing question instead. The moon shone through as the primary source of light as we continued down an area I wasn't familiar with.

"Boss, you need to tell her." The voice came from the driver's seat. "Yara won't be happy about this."

"Yara is dealing with her own mess." The warmth in Emilio's voice prior was gone. His tone was short, curt, *authoritative.*

"What do you mean?" Panic shot through me. Was she okay? The *bump bump bump* as the vehicle skirted off the road was jarring, but the driver quickly adjusted.

"Kazi, you should know better than to try to hide anything from me. We will discuss this later. There's a reason I made you stay behind, but Mateo will keep an eye out for her. Don't worry too much."

"How do you know Yara?" I pitched forward in my seat, trying to catch the man's face in the mirror, but it was shrouded in shadows.

"Isa, you didn't think I would leave your friend unprotected, did you?" Emilio tugged me back and over to his side, wrapping his strong arms around me. His muscles hardened as he secured me in a tight embrace. His head fell to my shoulder, burying his face there.

"Emilio." I struggled for a moment against his hold, but then the memory of our recent night together and of the summer all those years ago edged their way into my mind.

My body relaxed on its own accord, heat pooling between my thighs. My reaction had me once again questioning my sanity.

I had just seen a man's head explode into pieces.

Why isn't that bothering me?

"That's it, I'm not going to hurt you, and you instinctually know that, don't you? You're wet for me, aren't you? I bet I could easily sink my cock into you right now. Your body is always ready for mine."

I grumbled in attempted disagreement. But he was right. I was anxious and on edge but beneath that was unmistakable neediness. A comfortability.

I wanted this man again. My body recognized his.

But what about Oliver and Maddox?

He moved my hair aside to lay a single kiss on the column of my throat, directly over the mark he had left behind. “It’s been 10 years, my Bella Isa, surely you haven’t forgotten your promise.”

Promise. *Promise*?

I wracked my brain, trying to catch up with the information overload.

The vehicle slammed to a stop. Squirming out of Emilio’s embrace, I looked out the window.

A church?

“I was hoping for it to go a bit differently, but your two *friends* threw a wrench into my plans. No matter, a pact is a pact.”

Promise? Pact? Ten years.

Realization flushed through me. “Emilio, you can’t be serious.” I attempted to fling myself out the other door, furthest from him, but he caught me by the waist.

In my stupor, Emilio was able to manhandle me into his arms, and that is where I was wrapped as he carried us up the chapel’s steps.

It was a huge building that appeared to be hundreds of years old based on the design, but it wasn’t falling apart at all. On the contrary, it was clearly well taken care of, even the small patch of grass in the front was well manicured.

For a moment, I thought I might be in some type of fever dream, but when the driver, Kazi, opened the door, I could no longer deny I was seated in reality.

The pews were lined in rows and eerily empty, cast in shadows by the candles.

This was a scene straight out of a nightmare.

Why wasn’t I running? Screaming?

There were also hundreds of rainbow fairy lights adorning the walls, fresh flowers at the ends of the pews between the candles, and beautiful crimson stained glass moths hung from the large windows. It turned the nightmare into something...oddly soothing. Comforting. Someone had put a lot of effort into this chapel, but why?

Emilio tightened his grip on me, the rough pads of his fingers digging into my skin, as he walked us down the aisle. "Come on, Isa, it's past midnight. I waited the full 10 years as promised, but now it's time to follow through on our pact. We're getting married."

Chapter 4
Izzy

His words bounced around the chapel before landing across my skin. They burned me, bringing me to my senses.

My mind was a muddled mess of confusion, chaos, and apprehension.

He couldn't be serious.

"I'm not signing anything or agreeing to this," I argued, attempting to escape the confines of his arms.

Except he was much stronger now than he had been in our youth. I could barely budge.

Before, he had been a comfort–a salve needed after a traumatic night–but now I wasn't so sure. I knew Emilio lived a darker lifestyle, that his *family* owned most of this town, but he had always made me feel safe. Protected. *Loved*.

Emilio remained silent, but the chapel suddenly roused with an eerie tune.

A wedding march.

We were only half a dozen steps from the altar at this point, and he wasn't slowing his pace or loosening his grip.

"Emilio, you aren't thinking clearly." My heart pounded into my ears.

This isn't happening.

My head swiveled, searching for anyone to come to the rescue. But there were only the four of us here and Kazi was not going to be my ally. I found the priest's attention, but he quickly looked away, clutching a bible to his chest. He was muttering under his breath and his wiry gray hair was disheveled. Upon closer inspection, I noted he appeared to have been freshly pulled from his sleep. His garb was littered in wrinkles and his face still had the indents from a pillow.

Is he *even here of his own free will?*

"Emilio." I put as much oomph into my voice as I possibly could. "I am not agreeing to marry you."

"Kazi, give him the form to sign," Emilio barked out the order, his voice held none of its previous warmth.

Kazi came up from behind and handed the priest a single piece of paper to sign. Kazi shifted uneasily from foot to foot, his charcoal eyes flashing around in anxiety, his hands clenching and unclenching.

Emilio and I had made it to the altar now too.

"Son, this isn't right." The priest cast me a cursory glance, scribbling on the form, nonetheless.

I could just make out what the top of the paper said before Kazi wrenched it away.

NON-DISCLOSURE AGREEMENT.

It looked eerily close to the documents Emilio had me sign in the car.

What the actual fuck is going on?

"Neither are your ties to that abuser. *Stephen*. Or is it Steve now? You were given grace in our family, but you chose to go against our wishes. This is your salvation," Emilio snarled the words out, pushing the priest off the altar. "You have until this wedding is over to leave this town. *Go*!"

The priest's face turned ashen, and he didn't hesitate a moment longer before running for the door. I watched over Emilio's shoulder as the priest made it outside.

I was able to see two men in black suits grab him by the arms as the doors closed shut.

"Emilio, what are you doing?" My anxiety was hammering against my chest painfully. My unease weaved synchronously with my curiosity.

Emilio finally lowered me gently to the ground, keeping his much larger hand wrapped around my bicep. He turned to face me. His caramel eyes met mine. At that moment it wasn't as if time had stopped, but it was as if nothing else mattered.

We were transported back to when we first met.

When he saved me.

When we spent the summer together.

When I fell in love with him.

My resolve softened.

His free hand came up to cup my cheek, the pad of his thumb finding my lips. He pressed against them, forcing me to kiss it.

Emilio bent down until his lips were centimeters away from mine and spoke in his soft and comforting tone that he used to use exclusively with me. "Bella Isa, I love you. I have loved you since the moment I saw you all those years ago. There are a million things I could tell you, a thousand pretty lies, but here is the truth of the matter: I will spend every last breath showing you what it means to be enough. I will make you my priority in all that I do. I will ensure there is nothing left for you to fear in this world. I will keep you by my side through it all, I won't let you go again. All I need from you is to take a leap, to trust me. Can you do that?"

"I can, but—" Oliver and Maddox's faces slid into my mind. I couldn't do this to them. They were a part of my heart, too.

Correctly guessing where my mind had gone, Emilio's lips flattened, his voice turned guttural. *Harsh.* "I was almost too late, but you aren't with them. And if having those two in your life is what you need for your happiness? I won't keep you from them. But if they hurt you? If they lie to you? I make no promises."

My eyelids fluttered shut, and I squeezed them tight.

Fuck. Fuck. Fuck.

Was I really going to do this? Was I going to make this leap with Emilio? A man I hadn't seen in 10 years? Did I even truly have a choice?

"I do." *Have a choice.*

Just like I did all those years ago.

I could recognize that Emilio had planned all of this. From the burgundy moths to the rainbow lights. He clearly wanted to give a delicate side to this moment solely for my sake...

I didn't open my eyes as he sealed the promise with a kiss.

Now that I knew it was his lips pressing against mine–the *familiarity*, the *comfortability*–I couldn't help but think how stupid I was for not realizing it before. For not knowing he was the one that Yara sent to my hotel room.

That it was Emilio. It had always been and would always be him. I had always loved him, I had buried it, stamped it down, but it was there. A steady thread that pulsated along my nerves.

I owed him a large portion of my soul, my innocence, my mental health.

I may need to go to therapy, but I hadn't actually lost it *yet.* And that was because of Emilio, because he had saved me all those years ago. Because he had instilled confidence into me. Because he had always shown me my worth.

A million thoughts swarmed around my mind, but then he slipped something into place on my finger.

My *ring* finger.

"Mine."

Crash! Bang!

Behind us, the church's doors slammed open.

Chapter 5

Oliver

His Isobel

"I have located Isa. She is safe. I will bring her to you both. ETA two hours."

Oliver's knuckles whitened as he clutched the steering wheel aggressively. He sped down the back roads of their town, a specific destination in mind. The words from Milo echoed around his brain.

Why would it take two hours to return? Something wasn't right.

There was one place he knew he could go. One man that ran this town. He could help them.

The man *owed* Oliver after all.

"You're going to break it," Maddox stated, looking up from his phone.

"I don't *care*. She's missing," he bit out. "Why did we let her go out into the hallway? Why didn't we do anything to stop her?"

"Because she asked us not to, and we respect her wishes." Maddox shifted in his seat; he was almost comically oversized for the small vehicle.

"Emilio will find her for us." Oliver would be reunited with his Isobel.

No matter the cost.

"From what you've told me, that man is the literal devil of this town, and you haven't seen him in over 10 years. Who's to say he's even the man in charge anymore?" Maddox grunted out, readjusting again, his knees squeezing against the dashboard.

Oliver turned the corner, whipping the vehicle dangerously close to the sidewalk. Up ahead, the moon shined brightly onto a church that he was intimately familiar with. It was where he went for Sunday service his entire childhood. Where he first met the young Emilio.

Where his dad *died*.

"Something doesn't seem right. Why is it lit up like that? Isn't their business usually conducted under the church?" Maddox cut through Oliver's anxiety. The words ricocheted around the confined space of the vehicle.

Oliver wasn't sure what was stabbing at his psyche, but without thought, he swerved up onto the lawn of the church and jumped from the car.

Just as he made it to the steps, he heard movement behind him.

"State your business."

Oliver paid no mind to the unfamiliar voice; he didn't pause as he flung the church doors open.

He blinked his eyes a few times to adjust to the sight before him.

"Isobel!"

Panic. Anxiety. Turmoil.

Confusion.

"Get the fuck away from her!" Oliver was sprinting now, ignoring the candles on the ground and the familiar rhythm he couldn't quite place. The voice in his brain screaming something wasn't right.

His attention focused on Isobel's tear-stained face. On the man that held her, the man from the plane, from the reunion.

Was this the man who took her? Had Milo lied when he had said he'd found her?

Her eyes widened in surprise. He couldn't hear her, but he could see as she mouthed his name in horror.

He didn't understand. Nothing made sense.

Isobel stepped out of the man's embrace as Oliver reached them.

Oliver didn't pause; he raised his fist, pulled back, and swung it directly into her captor's gut.

The man made a satisfying grunt of pain, bending over, before Oliver was restrained, his arms pulled uncomfortably behind him by firm hands. The cool metal of a gun was pressed to his temple.

"What are you doing?" Isobel shrilled. "Let him go!"

"Boss?"

The captor stood back up to his full height, brushing off his clothes and turning the severe intensity of his gaze to Oliver. "We need to talk," he stated brusquely before reaching out and tugging Isobel back to him.

Rage percolated through Oliver's veins as he took in the stranger who held his Isobel hostage.

This must be who took her. A fucking stalker.

"You sick freak!" Oliver yelled the words, spit flying from his mouth as his chest heaved in and out. He wasn't in control, and his mind was unraveling. His good boy persona liquefying.

"You really don't recognize me? I'm hurt." The freak's smile was all teeth as he tightened his grip on Isobel.

Oliver had a moment of shock to see she wasn't fighting back before a new voice broke into the space.

"Ellie?"

Oliver turned to the voice, the pistol following his move.

Maddox was being pushed into the church, two goons at his back.

"Is this really necessary?" Isobel's soft voice was static with concern. "Oliver, Maddox, I need to say this first. I haven't made a choice, but I need you both to understand. And if at the end of it you want to leave me? You don't want to deal with this? I understand, but just know that I do care about you both more than words can express."

Her hand came up to cup Oliver's face.

One of the candles reflected off of a ring on her finger.

"What have you done?" It took a moment to realize it wasn't his own voice.

Maddox was no longer the docile prisoner as he fought back against the two captors. Swinging one into the other.

Without further delay, Oliver did the same. Reaching up to grab the gun from his temple and twisting it away.

He pivoted, delivering a bone-crushing kick to one of the men's faces. It was the man who had been holding the gun and it bounced against the ground a few feet before sliding underneath a pew. Oliver only had an instant of satisfaction before the stranger that had his Isobel launched off the podium at him. A fist finding his cheek, the shock causing him to take several steps back.

After that it was a chaotic mess of fists, kicks, and yelling that Oliver couldn't keep track of.

He was delivering as much violence as he could, allowing his anger and confusion to power him through.

That was, until a gun shot pierced the room.

Chapter 6
Izzy

"Butterscotch!" I yelled out as I lowered the gun from the air, my chest heaving.

Nothing was going right, this day was in fact pulled directly from a fever dream.

"That's enough." I manifested my most inner bitch, pulling from years of Yara's energy. I clenched my jaw, straightened my spine, and looked down my nose at the idiots.

"Isa, give me the gun back." Emilio lifted a hand, staggering from the foray of violence.

The rest of the men all paused.

"No! You fucking psychotic lunatics! All of you!"

My heart was beating rapidly in my ears as I took in the scene before me. From my vantage point, I could see the bloodied noses, bruised faces, and busted knuckles.

I was exceptionally aware that these men were brawling in a church.

I pointed to two of Emilio's men. "You two, go blow out all of these fucking candles before we go up in flames."

They didn't move until Emilio inclined his head just a bit. "You are to listen to her now, too."

They didn't hesitate a moment longer.

Is this what my life would be now?

I knew back in high school that Emilio wasn't a good man, that no typical teenager owned a gun, had a driver, and lived in a gated mansion.

After our time together, when I moved off to New York, I decided I wanted to know more about the man that had stolen my heart. It didn't take long to find the articles on his family's sordid past and their ties to the cartel.

"Ellie, who is this man?" Maddox's soothing voice sent waves of calm along my skin even from across the room.

Flicking the safety on the gun, I set it down behind me. As I sidestepped Emilio, elbowing one of his men aside, I found my way into Maddox's embrace. His familiar scent enveloped me.

Maddox was safety. Sanity. *Rational.*

His bulky arms extended out wrapping their way around me. He lifted me up, and I latched onto him. A needed life vest amidst a sea of chaos. My hands raised on their own, going to his face, holding him in place. Other than a split lip, there wasn't much evidence of his previous altercations. Meeting his gaze, we communicated for a moment in silence. I narrowed my eyes, raising one eyebrow. In turn, he sheepishly lifted up his shoulders and quirked his lips.

I pressed my forehead to his.

"You're sweaty," I stated attempting to ignore the embarrassment and insecurity that were squirreling their way into this moment.

"Isobel." Oliver's tone was harsh, unyielding.

"Dad is mad," I whispered to Maddox.

"Livid," Oliver grunted out, but he didn't move.

The only movement was of the men slowly blowing out the candles along the aisle. It was almost comical to watch. If it weren't also a stark reminder of why they were there in the first place.

Was I aware that I was in Maddox's arms in a church that I had just married another, admittedly dangerous, man in?

Yes.

Was I going to pretend like that wasn't the case?

Also yes.

"I think it might be time for a healthy dose of communication before we all kill each other. Besides, isn't that what is needed as the foundation of a healthy relationship?" I laughed the words out nervously.

"You're right, Isa. After all, Oliver and I have quite a bit to catch up on," Emilio responded before turning his attention to Oliver. "I can't believe you didn't recognize me, though I guess I was a lot smaller when we strung your dad up in this church."

What does that even mean?

My head jerked from Maddox, finding Emilio.

The latter was staring up above at the rafters.

"Emilio?" In all my years alongside Oliver I had never heard the absolute terror that saturated his voice before. "You're Emilio?"

Emilio didn't answer for a few minutes, his eyes focused above.

I tried to find what he was looking at, but there wasn't anything there.

Finally, he lowered his attention back into the here and now. "Oh, thought I saw a ghost," he said. "Isa, guide us little girl. Take us where you want before I slice Maddox's hands off for daring to touch what's mine."

Fuck.

What have I gotten myself into?

Chapter 7

Emilio

His Isa

Emilio thrummed his fingers against his pants in agitation. Seated back in his SUV, he wanted nothing more than to rip *his* Isa from *Maddox's* grip.

But he couldn't. He promised her that she was free to have these men in her life.

"Where are we going?" Oliver asked from beside him.

No, Emilio didn't get to hold his Isa. Instead he was leg to leg with the bane of his existence.

One of his first and most trusted allies.

The man that helped him to exact his revenge.

"To Emilio's house," Isa murmured out as she melted further into Maddox's arms. Emilio watched her in a haze.

It didn't look particularly comfortable to Emilio, but contrary to his thoughts, it was only a few minutes of uncomfortable silence later that Isa was fast asleep.

He didn't blame her, once the adrenaline wears off, all that settles in its dust is a bone deep exhaustion.

Isa let out a mewling snore.

Emilio bent forward to stroke her face, ignoring Maddox entirely.

"Why are you wearing wedding bands?" Maddox grumbled softly; reaching up to brush Emilio's hand away but Emilio was already settling back in his seat.

Emilio's dick was hardened uncomfortably in his pants. He wanted nothing more than to wake her up on his fingers again, but first, he needed to set ground rules. Establish his newfound unwanted acquaintance with the other men in this car.

"Look." He rubbed his temple and angled as far away from Oliver as he could, surveying both the men.

He was used to being the youngest, of others looking down on him for it, but that wasn't going to happen here. If either of these men fucked up, or hurt his Isa? He would kill them with his own bare hands.

He didn't care about the history he and Oliver shared. It wouldn't matter.

"I think before we get into that there's something else you both need to be aware of." He lifted his lips as if to smile, before baring his teeth at them. "You two and Yara all ought to look into vetting your security teams better. I'm Emilio, but you also know me by the names of Milo or perhaps even Emil."

They both opened their mouths in shock; Oliver's face whitening, Maddox's hold on Isa noticeably tightening.

"There is something else you need to get straight. Isa and I have history. She is, and always has been, *mine.*"

"This is what you were doing when I asked you to watch after her? Keep her safe from that asshole of a step-father? You were getting closer? Crawling your disgusting vines into her orbit? She is too good for you. You're a fucking killer," Oliver's hushed whisper did nothing to dispel the obvious vitriol he spat at Emilio.

"Aren't we all?" Emilio relaxed his shoulders, his head leaning back as he finally ripped his attention from Isa.

Everything Emilio touched turned into destruction. Bloody. Chaos.

That was why he told Isa he couldn't be with her. Why he promised her a summer.

One summer.

But then she said those fucking words.

"She loves me." Emilio didn't bother to look at the men when he said it. Those words had shifted the course of his life, they had upended all of his previous plans, dissipated his need for revenge.

He knew Oliver and Maddox wouldn't take it well, wouldn't believe him. They would have to continue this conversation when Isa was awake to tell her side.

"Bullshit," Oliver barked out. It was a harsh noise. Nails against a chalkboard.

Except, maybe it was just Oliver's voice. It *irritated* Emilio. Because Emilio knew Oliver wasn't a good man. Oliver hid behind his suits, his false smile, his pretty boy features. But Emilio knew the truth.

Had witnessed his depravity firsthand.

"I don't care if you believe me or not, it's the truth." He finally looked to the men, his hands going to his knees, he tipped his head forward as if to share a secret. "And let's get one thing straight here. You may not have known it was me, but I have been helping you 'handle' Isa's issues for years. Or have you already forgotten? The ex-boyfriends? The cameras? The tracking? All of it. I am Milo, remember? I know your dirty fucking secrets, and maybe you told her part of it. But does she know the lengths you two went to? The men that you had removed from her life? That you set up each and every one of her relationships for failure? Sure, I was happy to help, but you two were the ones calling the shots. Are you going to tell her about *Harry*?"

The last decade had been exhausting. Living between New York and Florida. Keeping tabs on his family and Isa. But it had all been worth it.

He hadn't managed to conquer the town, but he was already one step closer.

"You *wouldn't*, it would implicate you too." Oliver's eyes met Emilio's.

Bright blue, like a robin's fucking egg. He was the boy next door, an assuming assailant. It pissed off Emilio.

"And? I'm not the one that wrapped myself in a pretty package and called myself a good man. She knows who I am. She searched for me after we were separated, discovered my family's connections and *indiscretions*. I told her as much when we were together. Yet she still fell into my arms after I found her on that roof, just like I had all those years ago."

"The roof?" Maddox finally spoke up again.

Emilio surveyed them both.

They didn't even know that much?

He bared his teeth, his nostrils flaring. "Does she even trust you two? Or have you forced her to? Isolated her from any other *healthy* relationship. Do you think maybe without the two of you in her life she might have been happy?" Emilio was applying pressure to their nerves, doing his best to poke and prod at Oliver. He didn't like this version, he wanted to see the one he had met all those years ago. The one coated in blood.

"And what about you? How long have you been watching from the shadows like a fucking creep? Why didn't you do something, say something? What were you waiting for?" Oliver's voice was a knife scratching a plate.

Grima. Emilio had heard that word a lot growing up and it is what he felt now. *Disgust.*

Emilio heaved a sigh. They were almost to his home now, and he watched as the front gate swung open to allow them in. He always wondered if the gate was for his protection or for the rest of the town's.

"I promised her 10 years. She had those years to find a healthier, easier, *safer* life. But instead, she stayed in the lives of a *pretty* monster"–Emilio turned from Oliver and finally took in Maddox–"and a brute with a chip on his shoulder who has a death count longer than my own."

Maddox narrowed his eyes. "It appears you did your homework on me. I'm guessing you know all of the bits and pieces of my despicable past. And I understand that you are *threatening* us. I get it, but I am offering you this. I will trust you for Ellie's sake, but the moment you hurt her–and I know you *will* hurt her—you will see exactly why my death count is so high. Did your background check show how many of those were done with my bare hands? Do you know how to kill a man without your gun? Without a weapon? Don't play with me, *boy.*" Maddox's guttural voice was thick with rage.

Emilio couldn't help the laugh that burst from him. He had been underestimated for years by men older and scarier than Maddox. At this point, he found it hilarious more than anything else.

Maddox didn't have a chance to react before Isa shifted against him.

The noise startling her, and all of Emilio's previous annoyance from the men dissolved. Her eyes fluttered open a bit before she let out a yawn.

The cute soft noise cut through the tension of the car.

"Oh, hi there guys. You're all staring at me. Is there something on my face?" Said face was turning pink now. It reminded Emilio of when she told him she loved him all those years ago.

His heart beat painfully against his chest. He had missed her so much. The 10 years of being in her orbit, just out of her reach, were tortuous. Watching as she made mistake after mistake. But she needed to work through it on her own. Emilio owed her 10 years away from him and she had it.

But the two leeches she had contracted were not part of his original plan. No matter, he could pivot. While jealousy was crawling across his skin, an even deeper more visceral feeling was penetrating his veins. His body. His soul.

Love.

"Just discussing our future," Maddox reassured her, his beefy hand reaching up to cup her cheek as he placed a chaste kiss to her forehead.

Isa pushed into his lips, her features softening, a beautifully bright smile encompassing her face.

Emilio expected his jealousy to turn explosive, but he was shocked when something else entirely happened. His dick that he had finally gotten under control, grew to attention again.

Before he had time to truly put thought behind the nuances of what that meant, the car came to a stop.

"I'm calling Yara," Kazi stated before exiting the vehicle and slamming the door shut.

Emilio didn't acknowledge him. Yara was a pain, but he couldn't do anything about her. Isa wouldn't approve of that.

Emilio wondered if Isa would feel differently if she found out the secret Yara was keeping.

Because it was certainly going to change the course of their lives.

Chapter 8

Izzy

It was odd being back in the mansion I first truly became acquainted with Emilio.

Where I lost my virginity. Where we spent the summer together.

Where I told him I loved him.

My face heated at the thought as I relaxed into the couch, it was soft, plush, corduroy. A stark difference to what it was years ago.

Noticing my attention to it, Emilio turned to me on the couch, sliding closer to me. "You didn't like the leather, I wanted to make your home more inviting."

A shiver of need ran across my skin as his words tickled against my ear. As a distraction, I surveyed the rest of the space and noticed other subtle changes. Brighter colors, throw blankets, a pile of manhwas I'd read before on the coffee table. Before, his home had felt sterile, hardly lived in, but now it was warm. *Welcoming*.

Oliver, who was sitting in the armchair across from us, stood up in anger. It wasn't often I saw him this *bothered*. He was a control freak through and through, including how he showed his reactions.

"She is not going to be living here." Oliver threw the words at Emilio's face.

Emilio placed a gentle kiss on my cheek before separating from me. He rose up from the couch moving until he was toe-to-toe with Oliver, practically the same height, but Emilio was noticeably bulkier.

"Come here," Maddox grunted out from the other side of the couch tugging me back into the security of his arms. "They seem to have some history."

That was new to me, but then again, I was recognizing more and more that I had been ignorant to several facets of my life.

"You are still the same asshole—" Oliver was slinging the words out, but I did my best to ignore him.

Their bickering was irritating. It seemed ongoing and it was beginning to make me really anxious.

It won't be like this forever, right?

I fucking hoped not, but I could acknowledge we were all on edge and life's curveballs were coming fast and hard.

Is this what happens when you keep burying your feelings?

"Here's your phone, we found it on the ground. You scared us baby girl." Maddox handed me the device before burrowing into my neck. His next words were a breathy whisper, directly into my ear. "This is the man who left his come behind isn't it? Are you going to let all three of us wake you up on our cocks?"

I shivered in anticipation, rubbing my thighs together.

This was wrong, my reaction was wrong. But why did it feel so *right?* As if every horrible decision and tear shed was to lead me to this exact moment. On this couch. Surrounded by these three men.

"That's what I thought, but first we need to sort all of this out. Communicate as you said. But later?" His tongue lashed out against the rim of my ear as his hand moved to the nape of my neck, gripping me there.

An uninhibited moan left my lips.

"What are you doing?" Oliver's anger cut through the desire that Maddox was building shovel by shovel along my nerves.

Burying me in his essence.

Maddox carefully disentangled, offering a quick searing kiss to my lips, before turning to Emilio and Oliver.

"Are you two done now? We all have secrets, we've all been lying. But as Ellie so elegantly put it, the best way to a healthy relationship is a solid foundation. So, let's start with the elephant in the room. Why are you two wearing wedding bands?"

Emilio let out a long booming laugh, his head tipping back. "Isn't it obvious? We're married."

Apparently, that was the breaking point for Oliver.

"You son of a bitch!" Oliver screamed as he lost the last of his control. His face red, a vein throbbing in his temple as he launched himself at Emilio.

Crash!

Where was the fucking gun when I needed it?

Chapter 9
Emilio
His Isa

Emilio's tongue darted out to lick away the blood dripping from his lip.

"Are you both done now?" Isa's aggravation was prevalent in her tone, as was her worry. Her eyebrows creased in concern, her adorable nose scrunched up.

"I'll be fine." Emilio offered her a toothy grin.

Her face whitened. "Bloody. Red. Crimson. Is that color going to be a running theme in this?"

Emilio licked his teeth next, wiping away whatever she was seeing there before getting on his knees in front of her, his head falling to her lap. "It might be, but I will do my best to keep it from you. Now where should we start, my Bella Isa?"

Her soft hands came up on their own and found their way into his hair, burrowing there and massaging his scalp. He hummed a noise of appreciation.

He had kept it short since the last time he was in her presence. He only started to grow it out six months ago. For her. He remembered all the nights of her fingers running through his long hair. Of his head in her lap exactly like this.

"I missed you," he murmured adoringly.

Isa paused as if she hadn't realized what she was doing. "It's been years Emilio. And then you show up to collect on a 10-year pact, not offering much of a choice. And now it seems you and Oliver know each other? I am tired of being given half-truths, of being lied to, and deceived. I have been rolling with it because that is what I've always done. But now? I need honesty, Emilio."

"What do you want to know?" Oliver's grating voice came from behind Emilio, but he didn't lift his head. Soaking up as much warmth as he could of his Bella Isa.

Isa's hands started moving again, tangling further into Emilio's hair. "Let's start with how you and Emilio met."

"Church," Oliver said in a monotonous voice.

"Emilio, will you tell me please?" Isa removed her hands entirely, falling back into the couch as Emilio raised his head, watching her carefully.

He ignored the other two men in the room as he recalled one of the worst moments in his life; it was also the shifting point for him. He was 12 and following his sister at his father's command.

Camila! Where are you? This isn't funny anymore! *He screamed the words in his head at his sister in frustration as he hid in a bush just outside a clearing deep in the woods.*

Emilio had been looking for her everywhere. She had left a few hours ago to "meet" someone and his dad had sent him to follow her.

When he eventually caught a break, finding her car parked at the forest's edge, he made it just in time to see her stepping onto a trail.

For a while, he thought she was deranged, walking aimlessly into the woods, but then she had made it to a small clearing where a large modern house rested. When she let herself inside, Emilio shook with frustration.

What was she doing out here?

And why was he forced to follow her?

He tried to see her from the inside, but all the windows were covered with just a bit of light escaping around the curtains. At this point he hadn't delved very far into his family's business. If he had, he might have known better. Known that this was their enemy's territory, that he ought to call for help right away.

Emilio stayed at his spot behind the bushes just on the outside of the clearing, doing his best to stay awake. It was nearing midnight now and the moon shone in the sky, trickling through the foliage he hid in.

He heaved a sigh. This was pointless, she's probably meeting with a boyfriend.

He fell back on his butt, leaning against the tree to his left. He was exhausted; he had gone to school and then soccer practice and now he was out in the woods. He began to blink, long and slowly until his eyes stayed shut.

***

Bang! Bang! Bang!

Emilio shot up from his resting place. He didn't know how much time had passed, but the moon's light still trickled down.

He shifted just in time to see the door of the house slam shut. He went to yell at his sister.

But it wasn't her.

Panic, concern, worry.

It was three men. One of them stepped forward surveying the area and Emilio was able to get a good look at him. He was wearing a suit that was incredibly disheveled and sprayed in red.

Jullian McKell?

The mayor?

Emilio's heart was beating rapidly in his chest as the second man walked into the moonlight. He blended into the night, dark clothes, cropped jet black hair, charcoal soulless eyes.

Christian York.

Emilio may not have known much of his family's affairs, but he knew one thing for certain.

Christian York was a dangerous man.

At this point, Emilio was terrified. He sat petrified from his vantage point when the third man moved into view. All of him remained in shadows, except his eyes.

His cerulean orbs found Emilio's.

Emilio had never seen the man before and watched in abject horror as the man moved into the moonlight, his lips curled up into a cruel smile before he gave an almost imperceptible shake of his head.

For a moment Emilio thought that the stranger would give him away, but then the man broke their contact, gesturing for the others to follow him in the opposite direction.

He didn't notice that he was sprinting across the field until he made it to the front door. It was unlocked.

Pushing it open, he crept into the house. His hands were clammy, his anxiety slithering along his skin, his panic tangible as he made his way inside.

He ran down a hallway straight ahead until the space opened into a living room.

He wasn't quite sure what he was looking at, his mind wasn't processing the chaos of the room. The knocked over furniture, the blood on the floor, the half-rolled rug.

"Help her." The voice came from his right and he spun on his heel.

A teenaged boy was tied to an armchair with rope, blood running from his nose. "Oliver?" Emilio had seen him at church before, but they hadn't spoken much.

"Help. Her." His head gestured to the rug.

There was a stain bleeding through it, and Emilio unsteadily moved forward. His nerves were on the fritz, and he pushed down the voice shouting "Don't do it!" as he bent down to unroll the rug.

"Camila?" He fell to his knees. "Camila?" The word was a desperate plea on his tongue. His soul separated from his body as he took in the sight of her.

Naked, bruised, bloodied.

Shot.

"Wake up!" He shook her. She wasn't breathing, she wasn't moving, she wasn't.

She wasn't.

She wasn't.

He was too late. This was his fault.

He shrugged out of his shirt, lifting her and tugging it over her body.

Her body.

A sob wracked through him, and his vision blurred.

"I told her not to come here. Told her it wasn't safe. I'm sorry," Oliver clipped out. "There's a new power in this town, she wanted to see the meeting. He wasn't supposed to be here until tomorrow, but it was as if they were expecting her."

Scratchy, grating. "Shut up!" Grima.

"Call your dad. They are planning an attack. They want to take down your empire." Oliver shifted a bit, struggling against his restraints.

"Why are you telling me this? Why shouldn't I just kill you here and now?" Emilio reached for his forgotten phone in his pocket. Dozens of missed calls and texts. He read the last one. It was the promise that his dad was sending his men out on a search mission for both him and his sister. "Fuck!"

He stood, turning away from his sister. He couldn't look at her right now, he needed to figure out what was going on first. He looked at Oliver and stared into his eyes, willing himself to see any lies in their depths.

"She was my friend. My only true friend," Oliver stated the words coolly. "The newcomer and Christian made my dad hurt her... It was to secure his trust and allegiance." He heaved a shuddering sigh falling back into the chair. "They made me watch as she begged, as she called for me. I'm sorry."

Emilio screwed his eyes shut; he couldn't process this. "I am going to kill your father."

"I'll help." Oliver's eerily calm voice vibrated into the space.

Emilio's attention snapped to Oliver, regarding him. "You don't have a choice." He wasn't sure if he believed Oliver or not. But maybe Oliver could be bait.

After all, Oliver was left here tied to a chair. Emilio stared him down. He didn't see any lie in his eyes. Only regret, grief, unending sadness.

Oliver cared about his sister. About Camila. It was evident.

Emilio dialed the number of the one man that could fix this.

"Young boss?" A deep voice cut through the line.

"Camila is dead. The McKells are planning an attack with the Yorks and a newcomer at their backs."

"I will handle."

"Thank you. And Mateo?" Emilio strode to Oliver to help untie him, his mind made up.

"Yes, young boss?"

"Jullian McKell is mine. Bring him to the church. Uninjured."

"Yes, sir." The phone disconnected as Emilio finished untying Oliver.

Emilio knew Oliver wouldn't be an issue. Knew that he would need help to end this.

He couldn't look back at his sister. She would be laid to rest after her killers were delivered the justice they so deserved.

Emilio offered Oliver a hand. An olive branch. A promise. Oliver took it, standing carefully.

"You have my word." Oliver finally turned to Camila, taking in her body. A broken sob escaped him. "I couldn't do anything but watch. I'm so sorry sweet Camila. You didn't deserve this."

Emilio understood in that moment that Oliver meant it.

That Oliver had cared about his sister.

"Let's go." He turned from the scene, ice settling deep in his gut.

He might not have known too much about his family's affairs, but he decided that night, it all needed to change. It wouldn't be long after that he went from "young boss" to "boss."

  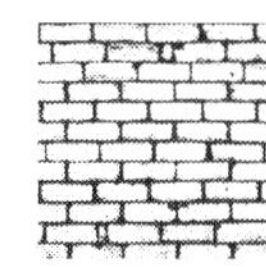

Emilio drew in a deep breath. "We did technically meet at church; his father was tied to mine, they had several *arrangements* in place. But Oliver and I didn't become very close for several years after the fact."

Oliver moved around Emilio and fell onto the couch on Isa's free side. "When we first met it was at my dad's gravesite, remember?"

"I do." Isa's voice was a melody, soothing Emilio's nerves. He did his best not to think of the night of his sister's death, but Isa deserved to know everything. Including what had first broken him, turned him into the cruel man he was today.

“Remember the date on the gravestone?” Oliver asked.

Isa nodded her head slowly.

“That is the day after Emilio’s sister died.”

Chapter 10

Oliver

His Isobel

"Well, then *you* tell her. The full truth, not the half-assed version. She can handle it."

Oliver didn't particularly like being told what to do, especially not by Emilio, but he was exhausted and didn't feel like arguing with him.

Oliver let out a calming breath.

None of this was going according to plan.

It was still dark outside, but not for much longer. They had eaten the night away with bullshit after more bullshit.

Oliver flexed his hands, looking down at his wrists. They hadn't scarred, but he could still feel the ropes from all those years ago, could hear Camila's screams.

It was the moment that had finally detached him from this reality. After years of attempting, of trying to be normal, witnessing the cruelties they dealt her was the last nail in his dead heart.

"When I was 16, I had a very good friend. Camila. She was Emilio's older sister. And without meaning to, I led her to her death. My father, along with two other men, tied me to a chair while they took their turns raping her. Each man fired a shot when they were done. Killing her. And that is where Emilio found me. Tied to a chair with his dead sister rolled up in a rug at my feet."

Isobel gasped, and Oliver felt as she leaned against him.

He looked down at her offering a smile, but it was in that moment he realized she wasn't wearing his shirt anymore. Oliver clenched his fists as a million scenarios of what had happened to her rolled through his brain. He had barely processed that he had to share her with Maddox. And now Emilio too?

She was meant to be his.

"Fuck man," Maddox grunted from the other side of Isobel, pulling him out of his spiral.

Oliver hadn't told this story to anyone.

"Due to my father's choices, Emilio and I agreed that he couldn't be in a position of power in this town anymore and when all was said and done after the fact, Emilio and I strung him up in the church. The official cause of death was suicide. The other two men had too many connections, we couldn't hurt them."

The irony of the mayor's death being less important was not lost on Oliver. His father had been larger than life. An abusive asshole that wanted more than he deserved.

Oliver didn't miss him. Didn't regret killing him. If anything, he wished he had done it sooner. Before Camila was murdered.

He took a few calming breaths focusing on Isobel's heat, the warmth of her skin. She was okay, she was alive, she was breathing. She didn't appear to be in distress. If anything, she seemed to be at peace. Or as much as she could be considering the story he was telling.

"This town was owned by two families. The Castillos"–he gestured to Emilio–"and the Yorks."

Isobel stiffened beside him, but he plowed ahead, filing it away in the endless questions he wished to ask her.

"That night when Camila was murdered, a third family was pulled into the fray. It was a necessity to secure my father's support. To show who would win if it came down to it." Oliver had played this conversation out in his head, a thousand different scenarios, each one with a different outcome. "That family was the Landons."

He had never expected Isobel to headbutt him with all her might. His eclectic Isobel never ceased to surprise him. It was why he loved her.

Maddox and Emilio started yelling over each other to admonish Isobel for injuring herself. Oliver didn't even bother, he knew she wouldn't listen.

Knew his words had upset her past her breaking point. Knew that the news of what he shared would not be taken well. Knew she needed to let some of it out, even if it was on him. Even if it hurt her a little.

"The Landons? My step-father? You fucking asshole! Why didn't you tell me?" she screeched, rubbing her forehead.

Chapter 11
Christian

"Where is he?!" Christian screamed at his men. He turned around and, in a rage, swiped everything off of his long desk. A picture frame bounced against the marble ground, shattering, before landing at his feet.

Using the bottom of his shoe, he moved the glass away to better see the image. It pictured three men–his brother, himself, and a *friend* of theirs. "Somebody clean this shit up!"

He heaved in and out, turning back to his five most trusted men.

Five. And not one of them could find his brother. Could tell him where the idiot had gone off to this time.

His brother, Sebastian, had just returned home and now he was gone again, off doing whatever the fuck it was he got himself into.

His phone rang, interrupting his explosive rage. It was their *friend*. "What did you find?" Christian snarled into the phone.

"A body." The voice spoke the words slowly, in his usual calm off-putting tone.

"Whose?" Christian reached behind him for the item tucked inconspicuously in his pants.

"Your brother. I just managed to take pictures before a *crew* was sent to clean it up."

Christian's heart pounded against his chest, he did everything to smash down the frenzied energy that was wrapping tendrils around his black heart. There was no love lost between him and his brother. But it was *his* blood.

Only one family in this town would dare to touch a York.

Even if the treaty stated otherwise.

"The Castillos," the voice on the phone confirmed.

The egregious disrespect would need to be dealt with. He had called off the war due to the severe losses on all sides, and they had come to an agreement. Clearly that was now null and void, and he would need to act, but first...

Christian disconnected the call; he had heard enough. He appraised his men. "Who saw Sebastian last?"

Four of the men stepped back, leaving one behind.

Christian lifted the gun in his hand that he had pulled from his suit.

The lone man did not snivel or cower. "Sir, I did as directed."

"You did," Christian agreed before shooting the remaining four men.

His last trusted man did not flinch as the shots rang out, nor did he react as their blood pooled beneath his feet.

"Now figure out why he went off on his own," Christian snarled, his attention returning to the picture frame on the floor.

Chapter 12

Maddox

His Ellie

This had been a rollercoaster of a night for Maddox. He couldn't decide which emotion was outweighing the rest but currently it seemed to be *shock*.

Oliver had given him bits and pieces of this town. Of the depravity, the lawlessness. How the former mayor, Oliver's dad, was corrupt and it sent the town itself into a downward spiral.

He knew that the Castillos were washers, cleaning cash to then push out across state lines. He knew the Yorks were importers and exporters of different substances. What he didn't know was much about who the Landons were. Or their relations with Ellie.

She never spoke about her step-father, or her mother for that matter, and Maddox knew better than to push her on those topics.

"Her step-father? You left her with a known criminal. And what? Assigned a watch dog? How do the Landons play into this?" Maddox wasn't enthused with this new information.

Oliver didn't answer him, it was Emilio that chimed in. "Sex, they sell sex. Strip clubs owned by the Landons popped up, but they were a mask for a much darker agenda. It wasn't long before I had to step in. Isa, you haven't seen your step-father much, have you?"

Ellie was not back in Maddox's arms where she belonged. "I'm tired. This is too much. I need to get away from it. Take a nap."

"I understand. The bedroom from before is made up for you." Maddox had previously noticed that Emilio's voice was much softer when he spoke to Ellie than anyone else and that was solidified now. It wasn't hard to tell that Emilio was a goner, that he was wrapped up in the web that was Ellie.

Maddox didn't wait for Oliver, he readjusted his grip and tugged Ellie with him up off the couch. This time when he lifted her, it was bridal style. "You may not have married me, but I am going to be the one to carry you over the threshold of the bedroom."

"Maddox," Ellie grumbled, but there was no heat in her voice.

She was noticeably exhausted, dark shadows materializing under her bright eyes. A crease had formed between her eyebrows earlier this evening and it hadn't smoothed. Maddox reached a free hand up to it.

"It's okay. Everything is going to be okay. No matter what happens, you have us. All of us. Now lead the way Ellie."

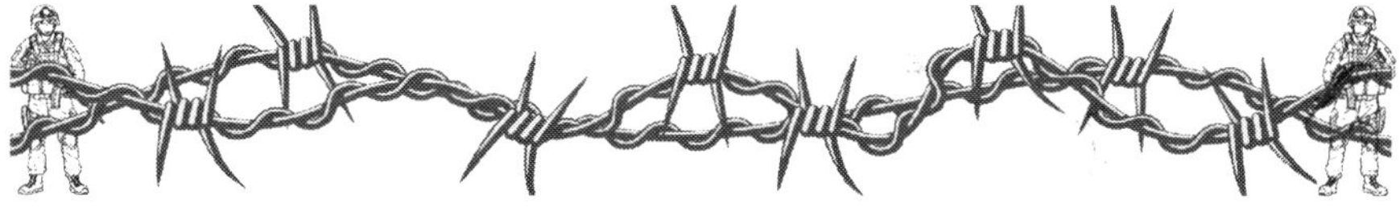

Ellie rolled on the bed to face him. They were in a room lined in bright colors, but with a blackout curtain in place. They had just made it into the bed after showering and changing into fresh clothes. Ellie was donning a sleep dress courtesy of Emilio, and Maddox was borrowing sweats. Now that they were finally stationary, he felt the weight of events settle on him.

"I love you, Ellie. I should have said it before everything happened, but it's the truth. And I'm not going anywhere. I hope you know that you're stuck with me. I promise to be the sane one as the other two make irrational decisions." The words almost felt misplaced, but he needed to speak his truth. It was his main regret when she went missing, that he hadn't told her.

And now she was married to a different man.

The thought sent vines of pain to wrap around his heart.

He didn't realize she was crying until that very moment. He reached out, tugging her against his chest.

"I love you, too," she hiccupped out.

The words solidified every moment that led up to this point. Oliver had been right, if all of this had come to light too soon, he doubted Ellie would still be here, in his arms. She would have run for the hills.

"Maddox, I can't fault you all. I understand why he kept so many secrets from me. I always knew certain things were off. I knew my step-father wasn't a good man. I knew there was more to this town than met the eye. But there's something I never told either of you." She was practically hyperventilating at this point and it took everything for Maddox to just allow her to vent. "My teacher, Sebastian York, he... he..."

Maddox heard the door to the bedroom open and close, but he was too far gone to care. "He what?" The room had turned a reddish shade as his anger filled him. York had hurt her? His Ellie? How? When? His mind was going a mile a minute, and he almost didn't hear her. And why in the ever-loving fuck was a York her teacher?

"He tried to rape her," Emilio's voice supplied as he sat on the foot of the bed. "On the roof of the school over a decade ago. That's how she and I became closer. I was already watching her for Oliver's sake, to keep an eye on her step-father, but then I saw she was becoming entangled with a York. I know that one stayed off the radar, but even still, I didn't trust him."

"That's why you avoid rooftops." Oliver was leaning against the door, his arms folded across his chest.

"Yes," Ellie sniffled out. "And I need you to know, that was when I fell in love with Emilio, when I promised to marry him after 10 years. He was there for me; he kept me safe."

Maddox had a million things he wanted to argue on that, but he kept silent.

"*Safe*," Oliver snorted sardonically. "Sure."

Oliver may have bonded with Emilio over Camila's death but they never became friends. If anything, they were enemies with a mutual tragedy that brought them together to retaliate, to commit murder.

After all, it was Oliver's dad that killed Camila.

"Sebastian's the one who took her from you two. But don't worry I made sure he was dead this time; he won't be rising from the grave again," Emilio confirmed, ignoring Oliver entirely.

Maddox breathed in and out a few more times, his mind spiraling in overdrive, so much had happened in such a short time. He readjusted his hold on Ellie, pulling her even closer into him.

She was his sole purpose for living, the reason he looked forward to every day. Before, he was an empty shell that had watched a child die in his arms. Lost in a world that didn't react kindly to broken men.

But now? He was happier than he had ever remembered being. Ellie had breathed life into every moment since he met her.

He would accept every piece that came with her. Even if it meant another man. Even if it meant two.

His mind was made up, he would be by Ellie's side no matter what.

Chapter 13

Izzy

I was hot, too hot.

"They wouldn't even let me claim a spot next to you after ten years apart." Emilio's voice cut through the darkness, but it took me a few more moments to gain my bearings.

Arms were wrapped around me on both sides, and I was in an unfamiliar space.

Before I could put much more thought into it, I felt the bed shift and then Emilio was maneuvering me up and off of it.

"You're going to hurt your back," I whispered hoarsely into the darkness.

"Shush with that."

Fully extricated from the bed, Emilio took my hand and hauled me through the darkness until he opened a door.

Instead of back into the main part of the house, it was to an outside opulent patio. The muggy air hit me, a slap to the face.

"I don't miss this Florida weather," I commented looking around.

The sun was rising and I guessed I had managed at least a few hours of sleep. This mansion was on the outskirts of town and all I could see in every direction was woods.

Emilio moved in my periphery and I took him in. He was only wearing a pair of boxers and his barrel chest was on display, ripples of muscles, broad shoulders, thick bulky arms.

He wasn't the same teenager I had been with so many years ago.

He was sexier, cockier, *bigger*.

But underneath that, he was still the soft sweet man I had fallen in love with. He was just in a harder package. I wasn't sure how to feel about it all yet.

"Come here." Emilio sat down in an oversized chaise chair and patted his lap.

I hesitated, but only for a moment before taking a single step towards him. It was all he needed.

In a swift motion, he reached forward and tugged me onto his lap so I was forced to straddle him. His strong hands burrowing into my hip bones, igniting a flame in my belly and keeping me steady. My knees dug into the scratchy rattan of the chair below as I settled onto him.

"This is crazy, isn't it? And your sister..." I examined him, my eyes taking in his face. It had hardened; all of his soft boyish features were now worn with age and it made him even that much more handsome. "You never told me what happened to her."

He didn't respond. Instead, in an impressive move, he bucked me up and shifted me so I was now lined up with his cock. I was bare underneath the Mumu I wore and I could feel his length straining against his boxers.

His lips pushed against mine.

They were fierce, unyielding, *treacherous*.

Addictive.

I had wrapped myself so far into a world of dangerous men that I wasn't sure what was up or down. I knew that everything I was doing was wrong. That this wasn't what others would accept in "polite" company.

But who fucking cared? I couldn't go back to my vanilla life. To the monotonous day-to-day. Not after all of this.

Consequences be damned.

It was time for me to live, to stop shaking in fear, always moving so safely.

Tedium had gotten me nowhere.

But here in this house with these three men?

I felt *alive*. As if I was not just going through the motions, but as if I was truly doing what I wanted to for the first time, *ever*.

I wasn't exactly sure how it would work. This had all been so fast, so incredibly jarring, but I was going to live in the here and now. Embrace every moment that I could.

I pressed against Emilio, further into the kiss. His tongue darted out as he claimed me, stamping himself into my skin.

One of his impressive hands found the nape of my neck, squeezing on just the edge of pain while the other made its way to my ass, underneath my Mumu. His hot hand against my bare skin, the rough pads of his fingers digging in, gripping me and tugging me even closer to him and further against his hardened cock.

I let out a moan, willing for the piece of cloth to disappear. Willing him to sink into me. I wanted to feel him again. Was our electric night just a one-off because the experience was new and exciting? Or was the way he had made me feel real?

Had I really stayed in love with him for the past 10 years?

After a few moments his hold on the back of my neck detached my lips from his, and I grumbled in protest.

"Listen Isa, I am going to fuck you. But first I need you to hear this."

Self-consciousness took this moment to scrape its ugly teeth into me, and instead, I shifted my focus to a spot over his shoulder.

The trees in the forest were swaying in the wind as the sun's rays slowly climbed to touch just the edges of their leaves. It made me acutely aware of how hot I must be, how it must be too much, and I moved as if to stand.

Emilio let loose a growl, a noise pulled from the depths of his body as he held on tight, not letting me budge a muscle away; it shook my attention to him. The vibrations from it went directly to my core and I unconsciously grinded my hips against his length that still pushed at me through a thin layer of cloth.

His caramel eyes were critical, striking. Analyzing me as if he could see my inner insecurities, my wants and needs. And maybe he could. He certainly had in the past.

He rolled up to meet me, his cock rubbing against me and I let out a soft moan. He was distracting me from the negativities that wormed their way into my mind.

"My sweet, Bella Isa. You always thought you didn't deserve the world, always felt the weight of other's attention and shortcomings. But not anymore." His sharp jaw ticked in anger. "We were apart for too long, and I was forced to watch as the men you allowed into your life hurt you. I may be the villain in some stories, but in yours? I will be your hero. I will be someone you can rely on. It's the world that isn't enough for you. And I pledge to spend everyday fixing your world until it fits you exactly as you are. I love you Isa. Every single piece and part. *Never* fucking change, not for me or anyone else."

My mind was a whirlwind of thoughts and emotions. Of how all of this was happening too fast, but then the realization that maybe this was exactly where I belonged. But how would this work, how could I possibly be with *three* men?

In spite of it all, there was one thing for certain, time may have left its ugly mark on my heart, but even so, Emilio still took up space inside of it.

I cared about him, wanted him, *loved him*.

I always had.

Emilio shifted underneath me and it took only a moment to realize why.

I hadn't noticed how wet our interaction had made me, how needy I was for Emilio.

Not until his now free cock slid up and into me in one plunge, fully distracting me from my thoughts.

"Fuck!" The word was a garbled mess.

"That's right, take it, take all of it." He bit his bottom lip as he used his firm hold on my neck to physically bounce me on his cock. Electricity streamed across my nerves as desire furled deep in my belly.

My hands moved on their own to hold onto his bulky shoulders enjoying the feel of his rough skin there as he pumped hard and fast into me from below. His eyes never left mine. The adoration is clear in their depth. It was edging just on the side of too much.

But Emilio's intensity was another aspect of the man I hadn't realized how much I missed. Another reason I should have known the man that Yara sent was him. He wrapped me up in every single moment, leaving me a needy and discombobulated mess in the best possible way.

I was a thousand tangled threads, and he was able to find exactly which ones needed to be tugged on.

"I"—thrust—"fucking"—thrust—"love"—thrust—"you!" Emilio growled the words out, not pausing his relentless assault. His hand on my ass squeezed tighter, just on the edge of pain. He readjusted his grip on my neck to the front and applied just a bit more pressure before his thumb came up to push between my lips.

Behind me was the unmistakable noise of a door opening and closing.

Emilio slowed his pace but didn't stop.

"Just like that, let me watch as you fuck her. I want to see her stretched out." Maddox's gruff voice was still coated in sleep.

Embarrassment and shame filtered through the desire.

"He likes it, Isa, just enjoy the fucking ride. Big man, show me what you can do while I fuck her."

"Turn her around." Maddox's voice was closer now.

Before I could truly understand what he said, Emilio was moving his hands to my hips, withdrawing from me and lifting me up simultaneously.

I glared at him. "What the—"

My words were cut off as he turned me on his lap, my knee awkwardly moving across him until I was now facing Maddox and he used his grip on my hips to impale me in one thrust.

"Just like that." Maddox ate up the remaining space between us before ripping off my Mumu. "Fucking beautiful." He fell to his knees at my feet, taking me in. We were, for once, at eye level.

I didn't even need to push down the stupid self-consciousness that I expected to wash through me. Instead, I simply *enjoyed* the weight of his attention on my entirely naked body in the light. By now I should know these men accepted me. Wanted me, every single piece and part, but it was still new. My brain wasn't quite on the same page as my heart, but it was almost there.

"Ellie." Maddox's rough hand found my skin, cupping my breast. His other moved to his mouth, wetting two fingers before moving it to my clit. "Perfection."

Maddox rubbed the sensitive spot as Emilio continued to pound into me from below.

Emilio used my hips as handles, his strong fingers digging in with bruising force.

"She is." Emilio's voice was a rough baritone in my ear as he continued to drive into me.

The desire that had started as an electric pleasure was building, the two of them working me like an instrument. Each man with his own part. Together they were shoving me to the peak, faster and faster.

Maddox pinched my nipple, *hard,* garnering my attention. I opened my eyes that had fallen shut in bliss and looked deep into his. They were swirling with thousands of promises, of a hundred unspoken words, of a future together just like this.

"Now!" Emilio growled the word out as his pumps became erratic.

Maddox focused his attention to my clit, rubbing heady, delicious wet circles on it.

Emilio's hands lifted me and impaled me.

Once.

Fuck.

Twice.

Fuck! Fuck!

And third times the—

Fuck! Fuck! *"Fuck!"* I screamed the word as I came.

Maddox pressed his firm unyielding lips to mine capturing the sound.

Emilio shifted behind me, moving my hair before peppering my neck with kisses. "Such a good girl."

"Mmmm," I moaned into Maddox's mouth before he pulled away.

Maddox's hand came up to cup my face. "I love you, Ellie." The words came out a fervent whisper, and I wasn't sure if Maddox even meant to say them.

Before I could digest my feelings and what had just occurred, a throat clearing pulled my attention.

"What the *fuck* is this?"

"Boss man is mad," I squeaked out, causing Maddox to chuckle.

Chapter 14

Izzy

The hot water from the shower was a necessary reprieve from an otherwise crazy day. Few days? I could barely keep track of time at this point. Oliver had not been entirely enthused to find me freshly fucked between Emilio and Maddox, but he had simply turned and left without any argument.

My heart beat anxiously inside my chest.

What if my worries came to fruition? What if by crossing the line I would lose the only three men I had ever felt such a connection to?

Emilio assured me he wasn't going anywhere, as did Maddox, but what about the inevitable jealousy? What about the fact that I was *married* to Emilio? Certainly, a rift would form and what about me?

My job? My life? Emilio had apparently followed me to New York, but his entire *family* lived here. I couldn't make him stay in New York forever and he even said that he made this place my home.

My apprehension was broken through by a vibrating noise. Shutting off the shower and toweling dry, I found my phone I had left on the counter.

Unknown caller.

I hesitated for just a moment before answering the call.

"Hello?" I asked with hesitation.

"Izzy." Yara's familiar voice was coated in relief. "I was so worried, nobody would tell me anything. Oliver said you were safe but then he wouldn't give specifics. What's going on?"

The background noise was *off*. Machines beeping, chaotic voices calling out. "Who is Kazi?"

Yara didn't speak for a few minutes. "How do you know Kazi?" The relief was replaced with paranoia. Suspicion.

I had never heard Yara sound so critical before. "Yara, where are you?"

Yara heaved out a sigh. "I'm okay, but I'm at the hospital. There's something I really need to tell you. It's important. But I need to say it in person, okay?"

"Aren't you back in California?"

"Not anymore, I'm here. Izzy–" A sob wracked through Yara. I had never heard her so heartbroken before, and I became incredibly concerned. "I'm so sorry, about everything."

"Hey girl! Hey! It's okay you have nothing to be sorry for. I love you, mamacita," I half joked, trying to calm her down.

It had the opposite effect, and she began to sob uncontrollably. "Please...please don't call me mamacita anymore. I'll see you soon, I promise."

On the other side of the phone I heard the distinct word *DNA*, before the line went silent.

"Yara? Yara!" Now my own concern was settling into place.

After a few nauseatingly worrisome moments, noise cut through her phone again. The machines beeping. "Izzy, I"—her voice broke—"I fucked up. Please believe me when I say I love you and nothing I do is to hurt you."

My mind raced with the endless possibilities of what had happened. Why was she at the hospital? What was going on? But at the end of the day, it didn't matter. I trusted Yara. "I love you Yara. No matter what it is, we can get through it together. And besides, I have a whole wild story to tell you as well." And I meant every word, but I knew in my gut that even though nothing I was doing was normal, Yara would support me. Just as she always had.

"Thank you girl! I will call you soon, I promise." That was the last she said to me before disconnecting the phone.

Chapter 15

Oliver

His Isobel

"You're an idiot." The voice cut through the darkness as Oliver stepped into the bedroom and watched his Isobel sleep for the umpteenth time.

It had been a week since he'd caught her between Emilio and Maddox.

Maddox he had accepted if only just barely, but Emilio?

The scoundrel was supposed to protect her when Oliver didn't trust himself to anymore. Instead, he had stolen Isobel's virginity.

It had only taken Oliver a few minutes to do the math, to figure out who it was. He knew someone had while he was away overseas, she had told him as much. But he thought it was a *nobody* classmate.

Not his *supposed* ally.

And to top it all off. Emilio didn't even keep her safe, she had almost fallen victim to one of the York scum.

It was that and the blatant disrespect that had caused him to spiral into his own mind. The darkness that typically lived there overcrowding the light that Isobel shined into it.

He was afraid he would hurt her, that he would say something he didn't mean. He needed time to wrap his mind around the fact that it wouldn't just be him and Maddox with his precious Isobel.

But Emilio would be joining the foray, too.

Maybe he should have taken her wings and locked her away years ago.

"Whatever you're thinking, no, just no. You have that sinister look on your face," Maddox whispered in a hushed tone.

"How did you—" Oliver protested before stopping himself.

Maddox always knew, even in their days together in the military. It was one of the reasons Oliver trusted him. The reason he allowed Maddox around Isobel at all.

"But what about the asshole?"

Said asshole was off for some *work* purpose but he would be returning in the morning. Ready to disrupt Oliver's carefully laid plans again.

All Oliver had ever wanted was Isobel and while he could acknowledge that he wasn't enough for her, that didn't mean he wanted to share her with two other men.

"Emilio is good for her. He pushes her past her point of comfort. Makes her feel good about herself. And besides, I don't know if you've forgotten, but they're married."

Oliver did everything in his power to control the surge of rage that rolled up his body, filling him. "They are *not* married in my eyes. Maybe by some stupid fucking piece of paper, but she is *not* his."

Maddox heaved a sigh, disentangling himself from Isobel's sleeping form, placing a soft kiss on her forehead before exiting the bed. "You're going to lose her. She has been on edge for a week. She already went through something traumatic and then a series of life-altering revelations. She hasn't touched Emilio or me since you saw us. She's scared, she hasn't said as much, but I can tell. Ellie was just starting to come out of her shell, to feel good about herself, and then you iced yourself out from her. You two have been friends for over a decade. Get your shit together."

Oliver clenched his fists and turned to leave.

"She loves you." Maddox stepped into his space and placed a hand on his shoulder.

There was just enough light in the room to make out the intensity of Maddox's stare. It was unnerving. "Yes, as a friend."

Maddox let out a humorless snort. "You're an idiot. Pull your head out of your ass before you miss out on the last remaining happiness in your life. What are you without her? Who are you?"

Oliver griped, "But that's the point isn't it? Emilio isn't good for her, but he can keep her secure with his army of men. He was her first love for fuck's sake. Her goddamn husband as you so aptly noted. And you? You're safe, you don't have any ties to the underbelly of this town. You're who she runs to when she needs comfort. But what about me? What is my role in this happy little *family*?"

Maddox dropped his hold before pulling his arm back and punching Oliver in the shoulder.

Oliver narrowed his eyes, his nostrils flared. "What do you think you're doing?"

"There it is. Sometimes I think you forget the mask you wear. You're what Ellie craves. To have her control taken. To be bossed around and told what to do. To challenge her. Are you going to ruin the only possibility of happiness in your life? Because I remember you on our tour together. You were a lost fucking puppy. *Isobel this and Isobel that*. You were goddamn annoying." Maddox smirked, stepping around Oliver and quietly pulling the bedroom door open. "But you weren't wrong. She is worth it. The obsession, the other men, all of it. I would kill for Ellie. Hurt anyone that hurts her. And that includes you."

Oliver expected the man to throw him out, but instead, Maddox walked out of the bedroom.

"Make her feel good." Maddox tossed over his shoulder, shutting the door behind him.

Oliver looked at his Isobel as she slept peacefully in the bed.

His beautiful butterfly. His darkest desire. His reason for life.

He stepped further into the room.

Chapter 16

Christian

Christian paced his office impatiently waiting to hear news. His *friend* had been residing in California for the last year, but he was remaining here for a bit longer in light of this emergency.

Christian knew that the treaty put in place after the mayor's *death* was a mistake, but they all needed to keep under the radar when he showed up dead. The cause of death may have been officially suicide, but the small town spoke.

A buzzer sounded on his freshly organized desk before his secretary's voice chimed through.

"Mr. Landon is here to see you."

Fucking finally.

He smashed the button. "Send him up."

Tugging the picture out of his back pocket, he stared at the image again.

His stupid fucking brother. His *dead* stupid fucking brother. This picture had been found in his effects. It was one of thousands. They all had one center of focus. One person circled. Two words scrawled out.

My Bel.

Christian recognized the girl, he hadn't been around her much, but when his *friend* got married to sell the image of taking up roots and being a family man, Christian had done his research. Just like he knew his *friend*'s daughter, Hallie, was adopted, he was also aware of his *friend's* step-daughter, Isobel. Why had Sebastian been obsessed with Isobel? Why did he have thousands of photos of her? There was nothing particularly attractive about her. She was too much for his taste and her face was boring, *plain*.

"Christian." The falsely jovial voice cut through his thoughts, and he shoved the picture back into his pocket.

"Steve," Christian acknowledged his friend, stepping forward and taking his hand. Part of him always regretted allowing this leach into his town, but it was too late now.

"It's Stephen now." The man's soulless cerulean blue eyes glinted in the fluorescent lighting. His features were practically angelic; a chiseled jaw, perfectly sun-kissed skin, blonde hair with not a single piece out of place.

It was at odds with who Christian knew him to be. Evil incarnate. Christian knew his grimy past, it had come out years ago. How he was on the lamb for harming his first family. Stephen had killed his first wife and abused their daughter for years before she was found and taken away.

Stephen's inherent immorality was one of the main reasons Christian wanted him around.

"Of course, I forgot you had changed it again. Is it still Landon?" Christian wasn't unaccustomed to the man changing names, Stephen did it just as he changed clothes.

"Hah, no. I've decided to go back to my first name, my birth name if you will, as I will be reuniting with my first family soon. I'll be going by Stephen Wick."

Christian decided not to question the eccentric man. The photo was burning a hole in his pocket, and he weighed the pros and cons of bringing it up. "Your step-daughter," he began.

Stephen's lips curled up, a disgusting replication of a smile. "Ah yes, your brother's obsession with her."

Christian slammed down the outrage that threatened to spill into his tone. He didn't want to get on this man's bad side. No matter how much he wanted him dead, Stephen was more useful alive. "Yes. Do you care what happens to her?"

"No. In fact, I have a wonderful idea." This time the grin on Stephen's face was real, but it was no less terrifying.

Christian's lips tightened at the corners, resolving to once more work with the monster. Christian's only remaining family—his brother—was dead. What more could he lose? "Do tell."

Chapter 17

Izzy

Warmth spread along my arms and legs. I felt wet. Sensual. *Familiar.*

This time in my sleep-addled state I knew exactly what this was. My brain wasn't fully awake yet, but my body was being brought to life by the hands that were massaging along it.

I didn't open my eyes or try to wake up, instead allowing the hands to explore me.

One moved to cup my cunt, large fingers pushing just at the edge of the entrance but not entering. The other stroked along my thighs, my hips, my sides, my breasts.

Both hands were being too careful, they weren't pressing into me or gripping me the way I wanted them to.

I rolled myself into the fingers that still teased at my cunt, willing them to thrust into me.

"You really like this, don't you?" the voice growled against my back, the vibrations shooting to my core in anticipation.

The person was wrapped around me from behind, their hard cock pressed into my ass, but still they did not take things further.

They were *teasing* me.

After a soft chuckle, the long fingers *finally* plunged into me, and I moaned my appreciation.

Keeping my eyes firmly shut, I willed them to push me to my limits. To take what they wanted.

I had told Maddox that this was okay, I had given prior consent to any of the three men in my orbit to wake me up this way, and I wanted this. I *needed* this.

A necessary escape from the realities of my world. From Oliver shunning my existence.

"Are you even awake or is your body just mine to play with?" His thumb moved to rub my clit as two fingers hooked into me.

Explosive shockwaves surged along my sleep numbed nerves. My body reacted to what it needed, to what it wanted.

In the darkness, half-asleep, was where I was the most comfortable.

There are no insecurities here, there is only want. Need. Lust.

Chapter 18

Oliver

His Isobel

He thought perhaps the first time they had woken her up, it had been a one-off. Maybe she would wear off of the novelty, but *no*.

She was enjoying this. Enjoying him taking what he wanted from her as she slept soundly.

Did she know what this did to him?

To be allowed free reign of her body while she slept? To be permitted to touch her how he wished?

Intoxicating.

But that's what Isobel was. She was meant for him. Every single piece of her. Awake. Asleep.

He knew that he would join her little harem of men, but he had needed time to accept it.

To realize it was *Emilio* who had taken her innocence.

Married her.

When it could have been him. He had come so close years before.

But he had discerned to give her a choice. Had promised himself to let his butterfly keep her wings. But what if she was offering them to him? What if she ripped them off and thrust them into his hands?

His fingers pressed into her wet cunt, reveling in how even half-asleep her body was ready for him. Willing him to slide into her.

She was partially awake now. Before, in the silence, it had just been him with his thoughts and an unsettling urge.

He had wanted to be quiet, *careful.* He had wanted to skirt the lines of what she had consented to entirely. Wanted to take from her more than she was willing to give. Wanted to fuck her without her waking up until his seed was inside of her.

For her to come to with the dull ache between her legs and unassuming soreness.

For him to leak down her legs as she began to realize what he had done.

But then she roused against his fingers, and the voice in his head shouting at him to break her softened.

Her moans overpowered it.

He hadn't even stuffed his dick inside her and he was already coming undone.

The thought served to both anger and empower him.

This was *her* fault.

He moved his fingers further inside of her, hooking into a spot he knew she enjoyed.

A soft mewl left vibrated out of her, and she stirred against him, furrowing back into him even further. He had discarded her clothes before this even started and the soft skin of her back was a stark contrast to his chest as she rubbed against him.

That fucking *Mumu.*

She had nearly pavloved him, now every time he even saw a fucking *sleep dress* he couldn't help but to picture her in it. His dick immediately stood at attention.

"Maddox," she murmured in her sleep.

Did she say his name to goad him? Surely she knew who he was. She should recognize him by his fingers alone.

He shifted his hold on her.

He had lost his very finite patience. He maneuvered, flipping her onto her knees in the bed, not concerned if she woke up or not.

"Wha–" She wasn't able to get the full word out.

He plunged his cock into her primed cunt. He had readied it for *himself*. Not for her. She didn't need to enjoy this.

But even as he thought the words, one of his hands found her clit, and the one soaked from her?

He carefully pressed against her rim of muscle. He had taken her virgin ass for his and he needed to remind her. That she was his. That everything about her was *his*.

Even if he was forced to make space for two other men.

"Oliver." His name was smothered by the pillow her face was pressed into, but he heard it.

"That's better." Maybe he would make her come after all. He sped up his pace, beating into her with reckless abandon. "You"–he pinched her clit–"will call me by my fucking name when I fuck you. Do you understand?" He wasn't sure when the monster had escaped his cage.

But here in this bedroom. With the moon cutting through the window as the only source of light. His beautiful Isobel filled with his cock, his fingers playing with her, she wasn't being fucked by the man she called a friend. She was being imprinted by the shadows that coated his soul, and only once his darkness had chewed her and swallowed her down would she be his.

Her moans had turned to screams, and he listened for her safe word. Because even a monster knew not to break her trust, knew to adhere to her wishes.

If only just.

“Oliver! I knew it was—” The words cut off by an incomprehensible noise leaving her lips.

It was *hedonistic*. It was his signal that she was almost there. He considered removing himself entirely, to punish her, but he didn’t have the self-control for that.

Instead, he slowed his pace changing to deep thrusts. It took *five* before she convulsed around his cock.

His own pleasure was just within his reach, static licked against his spine all the way to his fucking balls. And the pressure that had built against the dam? Her vice grip around him? Her broken voice as she cried out his name? It was his undoing and a moment later; he was filling her.

She tried to squirm off of him, but he held onto her, leaning over her back. “Oh sweet Isobel, I tried to let you free. Tried to keep you out of my web, but you’re stuck in it now. Are you scared?” His *clean* hand caressed her cheek from behind before moving to her neck. He gripped her there, pulling her up to him by it.

“No.” The word washed a sense of relief across his skin.

Anxiety that he hadn’t been aware existed dispersed into the room. Her one word unfurled years of doubts, of questioning whether she was ready for him—the true him—or not. “Good, now let’s get you cleaned up.”

Chapter 19

Izzy

This was a two-shower kind of day. Waking up with the soreness between my legs, my hair still damp, and stuffed between Maddox and Oliver had been mildly shocking.

But not nearly as surprising as the night had been. I knew it was Oliver by his voice, his touch, his hands.

Except.

My hands reached back, turning the water to a cool spray across my skin. It was helping to wake me up.

Yara's warnings came to mind, how Oliver had always been too close, too much. Too everything. How the way he acted wasn't normal.

Thinking back with a fresh set of eyes, I could finally see it.

Every coincidence, every happenstance, every time I felt eyes on the back of my head.

Oliver had already admitted as much, they all had. That they had been watching me, *protecting me*.

Is it bad that it makes me want them even more?

What did that say about me exactly?

I could joke that I really needed therapy, but I had a strong sense to realize that no amount of spewing my deepest pains to a stranger would help this.

I was obsessed with these men. Hyper-fixated.

I wanted their attention, it brought me to life, it sucked away every mean word a stranger had placed into my mind before.

Emilio's confidence—it built up my own.

Maddox's calm—it soothed my soul.

Oliver's control—it kept me in check.

They were re-writing my brain chemistry in a way that most certainly wasn't healthy, but I fucking needed it.

I *wanted* it. I *wanted* their attention.

The good, the bad, the *stalkerish*.

After all, if it weren't for their obsessive manner I would have fallen victim to Sebastian, not once but *twice.*

The name brought me out of my thoughts entirely.

Enough of that.

Shutting off the shower, I wrapped myself in a towel before going into the bedroom.

All three men were off on errands.

Emilio for his *family*.

Maddox for me.

Oliver for my company.

We had employees that had been calling Oliver incessantly, concerned by his sudden lack of appearance.

I was able to run most of what was needed from afar, but sooner or later, we would have to return home.

And then what?

My phone vibrated against the wooden nightstand just as I pulled my clothes on, I went to put back on my wedding band but paused mid reach.

"Yara?" I asked hesitantly. It was another unsaved number but not the same one from before. I wouldn't normally answer it except I hadn't heard from her in a *week,* and I was beginning to worry.

"No, it's your mother. Or have you forgotten entirely about the woman that broke her body to give birth to you?"

Mother.

Her voice was a siren in my ear, painful and loud. The last time we spoke was when she was admonishing me of my role in Harry's unfaithfulness.

"Laura," I acknowledged said mother.

"Back on that I see. I really wish you would make more of an effort after all the time I spent on you." She heaved a sigh as if this entire conversation was a tedious box she needed to check off.

She wasn't alone in that feeling.

"Well, I am calling with bad news." Her tone turned oddly passionate. "Your step-father and I are getting a divorce, and I need to see you today to discuss some matters in person."

Red flags and loud sirens started going off in my mind. My step-father. One of the "families" in this town. Had my mother known that she slept next to a killer, a *human trafficker?* It hadn't been hard to read between the lines when Emilio explained it.

"He left a year ago on business, and I was happy to just keep it casual, you know how it is, right? The house was a bit lonely, but I had my girlfriends at least. Now, here he is, back in town and demanding I leave. Threatening me. Telling me I need to vacate. The *scandal.*"

At this point I really couldn't discern what she was upset about, nor did I particularly care.

"Look, Laura, I need to go." I practiced my inner bitch using as much firmness behind my words as I could muster.

"Isobella Wright."

I stiffened as my mother called me by the name I hadn't gone by in over a decade. When I met Yara and I found out her last name had also been changed from what she was born with, I thought maybe it was normal to just change your name when you moved.

By the time I realized that wasn't the case, it was too late. I was buried so deep into my new life that I didn't want to look back.

"When you find a good man, don't let money get in the way. Maybe one day he'll do better," my mother sobbed the words out.

It was the first time I had heard her cry for as long as I could remember, but what she was saying didn't make any sense.

At this point the conversation had turned my emotions into a washing machine and everything she said was smashing the cycle button.

"What are you talking about?"

"Your father, James."

I sank back onto the bed; she hadn't spoken his name since she told me he died. Since we crossed state lines. Since she changed my name and made me promise to never talk about him. Never look for his family.

"What about him?"

"There's more to his death than I told you, but I need to see you in person. Show you the truth, or you won't believe me."

It was the only subject I would willingly meet my mother for. I rubbed my chest as the grief hammered its way into my heart.

I had never truly processed my father's death, she hadn't allowed nor helped me to.

Maybe this could be my goodbye.

To my mother and my father.

Because after this? My mother deserved no space in my life.

Chapter 20

Maddox

His Ellie

Maddox leaned against a concrete wall in what was most decidedly a dungeon. He didn't particularly enjoy this part of Emilio, but he could acknowledge the necessity.

Yara was missing, and they needed to follow any leads they could. So far there had only been one they could track down and she was ten feet from Maddox, hanging from a hook.

ELLIE: I'M MEETING MY MOTHER, SHE SAYS SHE HAS INFORMATION ON MY DAD. I'M TELLING ONLY YOU, I DON'T TRUST THE OTHERS TO NOT HUNT ME DOWN.

The text pinged through and Maddox did his best to keep his emotions off of his face as he pushed off the wall and directed to Emilio. He tried to call her but it went straight to voicemail.

Fuck!

Maddox was too far from her, he shouldn't have joined Emilio down here under the church. He should have stayed behind with his Ellie.

"I'll be back," he grumbled out.

Emilio stepped back from the woman that was dangling upside down from the ceiling, the one he had been interrogating for the last hour. The knife he held dripped blood slowly onto the floor as he turned to Maddox. "Where are you going?"

Maddox weighed his options. He didn't want to break Ellie's trust, but she didn't know the circumstances of what was going on. He hesitated for a moment too long.

Emilio moved swiftly, deftly maneuvering the knife to Maddox's throat. "If it has to do with *our* Isa, I suggest you speak. Or would you prefer I take the information from you?"

In this moment, Maddox could clearly see how Emilio had become the leader at such a young age. Emilio was naturally intimidating, his harsh voice eerie and off-putting.

Maddox's phone remained in his hand as he put it in the air in a mock of surrender.

Emilio's eyes landed on it. "Ah, I see." He didn't turn or loosen his grip on the knife.

Maddox could feel the blade dig into his neck, but he didn't flinch. He held Emilio's eyes, willing him to read his mind.

"Logan, get his phone!" Emilio barked the orders.

One of his men lurched out of the shadows to take it from Maddox before handing it to Emilio.

It took less than a minute for Emilio to find the message; it was clearly written across his face when he did.

"Her fucking mother?" Emilio snarled out at the captive. "Did you know about this? Know what he had planned?"

"You can fucking die! All of you!" The woman's screeching voice was only a bit wobbly.

Maddox stepped back from the knife before Emilio hurt him in a psychotic rage. He trusted Emilio...*mostly.*

"I know. I didn't expect her either," Maddox muttered, lifting a hand to rub his temple.

He was beginning to suspect their *lead* was just a means to get him away from his Ellie.

It had worked.

"I'll call Oliver so you can keep her trust. Who knows when she'll do something like this again." Emilio flung Maddox's phone back at him.

"She's going to be dead before you get there! I told him to use her mother. I hope she dies, she's a fat cow. It's not like you can kill me! My father wouldn't allow it, now let me go!" Those were the last words Hallie spoke before Emilio whipped around and threw the knife at her.

It landed in her throat, and with her hands tied together, she didn't have much she could do as she began to bleed around it.

"You weren't going to tell us where Yara was, were you? And now you have sent for *my* Isa? You want her dead? I knew you were evil, I knew you helped your adoptive *father* lure women into his clutches, but I thought you were a victim. It doesn't seem that you were, does it?"

Hallie spluttered, but Maddox couldn't make out what she was saying. He would have almost felt bad for the girl if he didn't know the lengths she had gone to for her adoptive *father*.

Emilio had explained the girl's role in her *father's* industry. How she had made "friends" in New York to bring them back home to Florida, only for them to go missing.

Maddox watched in silence as Emilio stepped to Hallie, retrieving his knife before plunging it into her heart.

Maddox hoped Ellie wouldn't be hurt by Hallie's death, that she would understand.

And it was in this moment that Maddox realized exactly how grateful he was that Emilio was on their side. Because when said man turned around? His eyes were lit up in amusement.

Maddox shuddered, he might have killed more than his share of men, but not once had he ever enjoyed it.

"Let's go, I can't believe they're using her *fucking* mother, or that it worked. They're going to take her, just like they did Yara," Emilio raged as he retrieved his phone from his pocket, calling Oliver as he climbed up the dungeon's solid steps.

A few days prior, Emilio had heard of Yara's disappearance through his men. Emilio had apprised Maddox and Oliver but they all knew better than to tell Ellie.

At least not until they could find Yara.

Maddox felt guilty in hiding it from Ellie, but he also knew she would just panic.

Except maybe they should have. Maybe then she would have been more careful. More diligent.

Regret pierced his heart.

Maddox spared the dead woman one last look, her corpse swaying in the air before following Emilio.

Surely his Ellie would be safe. She was *technically* Landon's family after all.

They wouldn't hurt her.

Would they?

But then again Hallie had been a more integral part of his family, and she had been left a sitting duck for them to take. In fact, it really seemed like she was used as bait...

Chapter 21

Izzy

My head felt fuzzy with a dull ache as I tried to piece together where I was this time.

I am tired of waking up in an undisclosed location, bound and blinded.

I tried to find humor in this situation, but how fucked up was it that I snuck out of Emilio's house to meet my mother and the next thing I knew, I was getting thrown into a van and my world went dark. That this had happened so shortly after Sebastian took me...

I didn't believe they were coincidences. But why would my mother lure me here? Had she lost her mind? Was she that bad of a person to kidnap her own child? And to what gain?

What in the ever-loving fuck is going on?

While I was most assuredly blindfolded and tied to a chair, my mouth was surprisingly uncovered. "Hello?" I called out softly.

"Izzy?"

That was not the voice I expected to hear. Confusion hit me in the temple.

"*Yara*?"

"Fuck, why did he take you too? Why are you here?" Yara's voice was coated in a deep unsettling sadness. Hopelessness.

"Who? Who took us?"

A door opened and shut to my left, a waft of cold air slapping against my skin.

"Ladies, now that I have you both. It's time for the reunion to begin!"

My blindfold was ripped off and I was suddenly face-to-face with a man.

A man I recognized.

"Him," Yara snarled from next to me.

I turned my attention to her. She was on the ground, her arms and legs chained to the wall. Her typically blonde hair was cut nearly all the way off in haphazard chops. And the bruises. Her face, her arms, her legs.

I wanted to scream, to cry, to run to her. My vision shaded red as anger pulsated through me, heating my blood and causing my heart to patter aggressively against my ribs.

What had they done to my best friend?

How dare they?

I was so caught up in my anger and indignation that I almost missed her explanation.

"My dad is back."

I whipped back to the man before me. What does my step-father have to do with her dad?

Confusion dug its way against my temples, the headache ramping up a notch as I tried to make sense of it all.

"Steve?"

"How do you know my dad, Stephen?"

It didn't make sense. How was this possible? This couldn't be true.

I wanted to deny it all, but the truth was literally staring me directly in the eyes.

It had been a while since I had seen Steve, but there was no mistaking it. He was Steve Landon, my step-father.

Chapter 22

Izzy

"How?" Shock was the predominant feeling that I found as my brain muddled, followed shortly by disbelief.

"How indeed?" the man hummed, stepping back to survey me. He brought a finger to his lips.

He looked like a typical late 40s working class man. There was nothing about him that screamed *violent*. Except Yara had said it was her dad and I had met her parents. Her adoptive parents that is. But this man? Now that I knew they were related, I could fucking *see it*. In their eyes, the shape of his face. I hadn't noticed before, because the similarities were subtle, but they were there.

But the tone that Yara had?

It was terror that this man induced. Her *father*.

It made my protective instincts latch on two-fold. This wasn't a good man; I had learned that much from Oliver.

What had he done to my best friend?

"I needed a family to settle in this town. To go unnoticed."

He swooped his hand towards me, and I wanted to flinch back, but I couldn't, I was trapped in this chair. I swallowed down my terror as it threatened to choke me.

"Why did I want to settle here? To keep an eye on my dear old daughter of course. Make sure she didn't forget my trainings, my teachings. She is my flesh and blood; therefore I have a duty to watch over her."

My thoughts were racing a mile a minute. My emotions were not keeping up as this horror played out before me.

Yara had never met my step-dad. She never came over to my house as he didn't permit guests. He hadn't really been around that much to begin with. I had probably seen him a grand total of 10 times throughout his and my mom's marriage. But I chalked that up to his job.

Except I had never really known his job, never cared to.

"But Hallie? Is she Yara's—" I don't know why that's where I landed, but I wanted to grasp onto something that made sense.

"No, that bitch is a falsified adoption. I needed a good cover, easier to lure a wife in with a daughter of my own. Though I don't think your mother would have cared either way." He pitched forward his finger, pinching my chin painfully. "I told her to teach you better. To whip you into shape. But you always were a cow. A disgrace. I was almost at the point of discarding you, but then you left town, saving me the time." He jerked back suddenly, slapping me across the face.

My cheek stung and the impact pushed my skin into my teeth. Copper filled my mouth, but I stared at him unblinkingly.

Hallie. Adopted?

My own mother... After all the vitriol she had spit my way over the years. It wasn't even that surprising to hear she had married a literal monster.

Except if they both hated me so much, why was I even here? What could they possible want from me?

My mind was a fuzzy mess.

I wanted to scream, to rage, and spew every curse I had ever known, but it wasn't only my life at stake. Yara was here too. I had to think of her. If we could just hold on a bit longer...

Emilio, Maddox, and Oliver would be here soon. I had no doubt about that. I just needed to keep my cool.

Because Yara? She was scared.

She had been there for me for so many years. Did we keep secrets from each other? Yes. But I trusted her with my life and in this moment I would be strong enough for the both of us.

Even if every nerve in my body was willing me to scream, to melt into a puddle of anxiety.

I wouldn't. I couldn't.

I needed to be strong for the both of us.

"But even a cow can be a whore can't they? Sebastian York took a fancy to you, didn't he? And then he got killed. But no matter. Today we can all exact the revenge we deserve."

My step-father, correction–Yara's dad, correction–Steve, correction—

Fuck, the *stranger, Stephen*, stepped back from me. During his entire spiel he had never raised his voice, it had been an eerie monotone. And even now, he wasn't frowning, instead he had the remnants of a smile in place.

It was disconcerting, but I pushed it along with my uneasiness to the bottom of my pile of concerns.

"Bring him in." Stephen didn't turn, his eyes watching my face intently. "It's time for your reunion."

Chapter 23

Emilio

His Isa

"Stop pacing," Maddox grumbled out to Oliver.

Emilio looked up from his computer as he flipped through the security cameras of the town. He had a team of men scouring for sight of Isa too, but he didn't trust others to find her.

He would recognize her even if her face was covered, even if only parts of her were visible.

Emilio reached into his pocket, clenching the ring in it.

The tracker in her wedding band was working, except she had taken it off.

He would need to fix that feature soon. The ability to remove it made it practically useless in his mind. Just as ineffective as Maddox and Oliver tracking her phone. The device had been found only a bit further on their search, on the street in front of their house.

"I need to tell you both something, I was giving Yara time to do so, but then she was taken." Emilio didn't look up from the screen as the two men squabbled amongst each other. While they were seemingly useless at this moment, he knew when the time came, they would risk their lives for their girl.

Because, after all, she was all of theirs. They would all do anything for Isa.

She was more important to each of them than anything else. It was the only reason this "relationship" was going to work. It was why Emilio allowed them in her orbit.

Sometimes, like now, he would need help to keep her safe, and he couldn't trust just anyone to the task.

"What?" Oliver seethed the word, stomping to just on the other side of the computer screens.

Grima.

Emilio ignored him, hoping one day to grow accustomed to Oliver's grating voice. Or perhaps it was the trauma. That the first time he had truly heard Oliver's voice was after those men had *killed* his sister.

He would not let the same fate befall his Isa. He would not fail her.

Smothering the anguish that squeezed his lungs, he refocused on the task at hand, clicking to shift a specific camera for another angle at the street. He had just seen a plate-less van drive by in the image. It was approximately two hours ago, so the lead might be cold, but it was a start nonetheless.

"As I told you, I sent one of my men to watch over Yara, and I also secured my spot as head of her security in order to have access to her database."

"We know," Maddox confirmed in his calming voice.

Emilio hadn't quite gotten a read on Maddox, but he had witnessed his devotion to Isa. How comfortable he had made her when she was in distress. How he had resolved the issue with the idiotic Oliver. And that was what was important. Keeping Isa happy.

"Recently I sent another to help combat a stalker that had set his sights on her. In the meantime, she met a man through her dating site. At first, I didn't think too much of it, but then I realized there was an odd familiarity to the man. And then I discovered what my men, what Kazi and Mateo, were hiding from me." His men thought he wouldn't be happy with Yara's choice in a lover, they were afraid Emilio might lash out, might hurt their girl.

They were wrong.

In fact, he was very pleased with who they had found in California.

Emilio clicked through the images, finally finding what he was looking for.

A man being shoved into the building. His eyes staring directly at the camera.

Now that he knew the connections to everyone, it was easier to find a trail.

The captive's familiar sage green eyes; his Bella Isa's eyes. They didn't even need to be on her face for Emilio to recognize them.

"Spit it out."

Emilio read a message from Logan before sending one off to Kazi and Mateo.

LOGAN: FOUND YARA'S ORIGINAL BIRTH CERTIFICATE AS REQUESTED - FATHER LISTED AS STEPHEN WICK - ASSUMED DEAD - HERE IS PHOTO

Just as Emilio had suspected. The photo Logan sent was unmistakably that of Steve Landon. They were one in the same.

It was all coming together now.

Proof.

Emilio finally gave his attention to the men, standing up from the desk and walking around it.

Emilio wasn't exactly sure how to say it. "In California, Yara became entangled with a man. His name is James, and he's Isa's biological dad."

He didn't pause for a reaction, securing his gun and handing one to each of the men.

Oliver's mouth was open in shock as he took the weapon, but Maddox's brow was furrowed as if it made sense to him. He stepped around the men. There was no time to spare.

"And Isa's step-dad? Steve Landon?" Emilio cast over his shoulder, divulging the news his second in command, Logan, had just informed him of. "That would be Yara's bio father."

He didn't want to think what that meant for his Isa, how she wouldn't be his target, but how she could easily be his collateral.

Just as he didn't want to think about how Christian York was angry, alone, and *on a rampage for his revenge.*

Chapter 24

Izzy

My step-father—no, his name was Stephen. He turned to the side, allowing me an unobstructed view of what was behind him.

Of the newest prisoner to join our foray.

"Dad?" my voice broke.

I can't be strong. This isn't happening. This can't be real.

He can't—

How is—

But that means—

I grieved for my dad for more than half my life. He can't be alive. I didn't even look *for him. I didn't even try to find him. I just trusted my* mother. *A fool I was, a fucking idiot.*

My ears pounded painfully as regret sliced through my brain attempting to break me apart.

I couldn't let it.

Fuck. Fuck! FUCK!

"Isobella?" James, my *dad*, broke through the chaotic noise of my mind unraveling. He attempted to escape his restraints, but the two men holding him overpowered his attempts. My dad's voice was a memory that pulsated to the front of my mind.

A hundred times he said my name in that exact way after I had hurt myself. When he came home from work and found me crying. I never told him how mom was when he was gone. I didn't want to worry him.

And then he died.

That hadn't been true?

My mother had lied to me? About my dad *dying?* What kind of sick, fucked up—

My mind unraveled as every excuse I told myself about my mother fell apart. She didn't love me, she didn't do anything for my sake. She was *evil*, *selfish*, a raging fucking cunt.

She had taken me from my dad. From the man that had raised me. Had loved me. Had taught me to be strong.

My vision blurred as tears fell on their own accord.

I didn't want to cry here, I didn't want to show weakness.

I wanted to be strong.

But seeing my dad in this situation after years apart was my undoing.

"Finally, together at last. Are those tears of joy? I can't believe your sweet mother isn't here for the reunion." Stephen snapped his fingers and rattling echoed around the room. "When she drunkenly told me what she had done? I grew curious. How could I use this secret? Because that's what it was–a dangerous and powerful secret. I think I did the best I could with it. But imagine my surprise when I sent James to lure Yara back to me and instead? He *falls* for her. He *fucks* her. He—"

"Stop it!" Yara, who had been uncharacteristically silent, broke, interrupting her *father's* speech.

Through it all, I stared at my own father, at James. At my long-lost dad. As the confusion marked his face. A mix of a furrowed brow and his lips pressed into a harsh line.

He had aged, but he was still unmistakable. His mannerisms. His voice. His eyes.

They were a mirror to my own.

Stephen's words eventually processed.

My dad and *Yara?*

I broke my stare down and diverted my attention towards Yara. The wall behind her was opened up. Before, it was panels, but now, it was a glass pane that I could see through.

My mother stood on the other side.

I couldn't hear her, but I recognized her expression. She wasn't scared, she was *livid.* Her temple pulsating with rage, her eyebrows raised to her hairline, as she began to wave her hands above her.

It was clear she couldn't see us, though, as she kept turning her head. She didn't focus in any direction as she continued her tantrum.

I flinched back, years of being on the receiving end of her anger had left a wound. Another reason I kept my distance.

Was it weird that I was grateful for the wall's separation?

Except... What was this? What was Stephen's angle?

I did my best to stamp down the shock of the series of events that had played out, I would process this. When I wasn't being held captive. When all was said and done.

Shifting back, I refocused on *Stephen.* Examining him, I tried to garner *any* information I could.

"Well, this hasn't been quite as amusing as I wanted it to be. Maybe it's time to spice up the party. Isobella. Who do you love better? Your mom or your dad? We always have a favorite don't we?"

Even now, knowing that the man speaking was a tangibly bad man.

I couldn't tell.

Stephen was a blank wall. An empty palate. A Skinwalker.

I didn't want to answer his question, but my eyes flickered to my dad. To the man who raised me into my early teenage years. To the man I had missed more than I realized.

To the man who I had an endless list of questions for.

"That's what I thought. I don't blame you, your mother is rather difficult."

Bang! Bang! Bang!

I knew exactly what gun shots sounded like.

I braced, willing myself to turn towards the noise. It came from behind me, from Yara's direction.

My dad snapped at me. "Isobella, do not look. You don't need to see it."

I instinctively listened to him, but I needed to make sure my best friend was okay. "Yara?"

"I'm fine," she murmured. I could barely make out the "for now."

My step-father huffed, gesticulating into the air, and a moment later, the same rattling from earlier filled the space. Two of his men stepped forward, one of the beefy goons kept a tight hold of my shoulders while the other untied me.

"Since you're a coward, I'll just rip the bandage off. Your mom's dead, she was just shot because you chose your dad over her. Now time to say goodbye to your dad and Yara. This will be the last time you see them both alive." There wasn't any inflection in Stephen's tone. He could have been discussing the weather for how he sounded.

I didn't acknowledge his words. I didn't process them. I needed to emotionally detach from anything else he said.

My mother wasn't dead.

I swallowed down the bile that came up my throat.

My dad wasn't alive.

I breathed in the musty air.

My best friend wasn't in grave danger.

I squeezed my eyes shut, scrunching my nose.

I whipped my head back and forth as I shook it, emptying my mind of anything and everything I could.

I repeated the lies in my mind, attempting to believe them.

"I'm sorry!" Yara screamed. "I'm so sorry Izzy. I love you!"

Her terror, her agony, her sadness. It broke through my mantra. It ate me alive. I wanted nothing more than to save her at this moment.

But I was helpless. Just like I had been with Sebastian.

I knew Maddox, Oliver, and Emilio would come for me. But would it be too late?

My dad grunted in pain and I whipped my eyes open.

James fought against his captors, but just like before, it was fruitless. "I will see you again, we both will. I love you, I never stopped looking for you."

"I love you too." I spoke the words to both of them, turning to get one final look at my best friend.

"Oh shut the fuck up!" Stephen lost his cool and the last I felt was the hard metal of a gun hitting me against the back of my head—*that's going to leave a mark*—before the world went dark again.

Chapter 25

Izzy

Agony. I am in pain. Everything hurts.

It was in this moment, on the cusp of being awake and still asleep, I realized how much I enjoyed waking up on fingers as opposed to...

Whatever the fuck this was.

That's it Izzy, cope through your trauma with humor. Laugh so you can't cry.

Because all I wanted was to break down. My head was throbbing a beat to my heart, my mouth tasted like tuna salad that had been left on the counter for a week, and my arms were *numb*, tingling with phantom pain.

They were tied down again. Except this time, it was just my wrists tied, extending on each side of me, and instead of on a chair, the surface beneath me was soft.

A bed.

Fuck. Fuck. Fuck.

The mattress shifted before a hot weight pressed down onto my chest, constricting my air.

It was time, I couldn't delay this reality any longer.

I opened my eyes.

And I screamed.

Sebastian? How?

"Hear that men? She's scared at just the sight of me. Or perhaps it's because you think you're seeing a ghost?"

Black treacherous eyes, hair just as dark but touched in grey that fell in waves into his face as he swooped down, his mouth centimeters from mine. He paused before touching me, his lips tugged up into a sinister smile before leaning back and headbutting me with all his might.

The pressure was a thousand explosions of fireworks ricocheting around my skull. Lights danced throughout my vision. I felt the heavy tendrils of subconsciousness pull me back into its depths, but I couldn't allow it.

I didn't want to wake up to these men fucking me or doing whatever the fuck they would do. Or what if I didn't wake up at all? What if I just died?

Shutting down that line of thought, I tugged at my restraints again. My right wrist didn't budge, but my left one?

Moving my fingers around, I felt a frayed part of the rope.

Hope infiltrated my panic.

I could do this.

I *would* do this.

"I'm not a ghost. Just the brother of a man that died because of you."

Of course it fucking was. Sebastian is dead. I watched his head obliterated in front of me.

I still haven't even had the time to process that yet.

"So how about this weather?" The question escaped me raspily before I could take it back. The line my *father* had instilled into me. It was a coping mechanism. I had used it countless times prior in anxiety, and now here I was spewing it at my would-be killer.

I had one moment of satisfaction where absolute confusion flickered across his face before it settled back. His lips quirked at the corners in a smug grin.

He bowed down, whispering into my ear, "The forecast doesn't look good." His disgustingly hot breath was slimy as it fanned me. "At least not for you."

I wanted to lose my cool, to dissolve into a useless puddle, to scream and cry, but that wouldn't help.

Yara needs *me*, my dad needs *me*. My men. They will kill each other without *me*. I need to be okay for them. For my job. I'm going to kill this mother fucking asshole, just like I should have killed his brother.

It wasn't my time to go, I had just found everything I needed to truly be happy. And I was determined to be fucking *happy*. I fucking deserved it.

I would make it out of this alive.

The smell of cigarettes permeated my nostrils and I surveyed the room as best I could. What I needed to do was come up with a plan. Because it was time for me to save myself.

Emilio had taken care of Sebastian for me, but now it was my turn. Maybe this was the universe's fucked up way of giving me a do-over. Of letting me exact my own revenge. I would be strong, I would escape this York brother on my own.

If only to prove I could.

Chapter 26
Christian

Why couldn't Sebastian stalk a less connected woman?

The step-daughter of a Landon with ties to the Castillos and *the McKells.*

Christian stared down at the woman. She was...*weird*.

She wasn't crying, or asking for help, or screaming.

She was fucking humming and it was annoying the shit out of him.

"You can leave now; I will call you back if needed," he directed the three men in the room with them. He could manage one girl by himself.

What was she going to do? Kill him with her off-key humming?

He waited for them to leave before refocusing his attention on the woman below. He still laid atop her, his weight compressing down onto her body.

"You are the reason my brother died," he reminded her, grabbing her by the throat and pressing her further into the bed.

He pushed his lips to her. They were soft, but otherwise, not noteworthy.

"I don't see the fucking fascination. A plain fucking woman. How did you attract my brother? He doesn't typically go for women like you."

"You mean women my age?" she coughed out, her throat moving against his hand.

He felt oddly calmed by the feeling of her skin on his palm. His grip on her, the complete control he had over her. He appraised her, trying to see her from a different angle, but he couldn't. There was nothing special about her ... Except there was definitely something disturbing about this woman. He just couldn't pin-point what it was exactly.

"You did know my brother."

He relaxed his grip on her neck, allowing her to gulp in a few breaths of air. He leaned back, his knees digging into the mattress on each side of her hips.

He hadn't expected to exact his vengeance so soon, but she wasn't the revenge. She was a tool to it. Christian had learned of the depth of her ties to the Castillos, of who had really shot and killed his brother.

It was none other than Emilio himself.

"Answer my question."

He watched her face, her cheeks were pink from her coughing, her lips puffed and swollen, but still she didn't appear *scared*. And her eyes? They pierced into his, striking and *clear*. As if they could see through him. He didn't fucking like them. He reached for a knife on the table next to them, moving the blade to her neck. He needed her to beg, to cry, to plead for her life.

But she just watched him with her unnerving eyes.

This wasn't fun like he had thought it would be.

"He was my teacher in high school," she spoke slowly, still staring at him.

Christian's mind raced. In high school? From what he had gathered, she was nearing 30. That's how long his brother had known her? And if that was the case...

"Do you know what happened to him 10 years ago?" His memory pulled forth the night from over a decade ago when Sebastian had called, and Christian had raced to him.

Found his brother shot and covered in blood on the school's roof. But his brother had never told him *why,* and then one day several years later, Sebastian up and left town.

Christian already knew at that point about his brother's proclivities. Had already started to clean up his messes. Tied up all the loose ends so that their image wasn't ruined. It was hard to make connections to prominent businessmen with documented transgressions.

They had to stay on the up and up for their empire to run smoothly.

"He tried to rape me, so I shot him. I moved away but then he followed me. None of this was my fault. You clearly knew who your brother was. It was self-defense," she stated the words matter-of-factly.

He thought he knew exactly who his brother was, but this woman was an outlier. Too old for his interests, and yet, Sebastian had been obsessed with her.

Sebastian, what were you thinking? You threw your entire life away for this woman?

Christian's mind was made up. While he could appreciate the woman's tenacity, she wouldn't be allowed to live. He needed to wrap up the remaining unfinished business that his brother had left behind. Sebastian's one last living victim. Because if anyone found out his brother's offenses?

Well, Christian couldn't have that happening.

Chapter 27

Izzy

I could see the moment Christian decided to kill me. It was almost imperceptible, but I was looking for it.

It was the exact look Sebastian had when he decided to rape me the first time.

There was no denying their relation.

Except I had a plan, I wasn't sure if it would work, but while I hummed away and Christian interrogated me, I had managed to loosen the ropes on one of my wrists.

I had found where the smoky smell was coming from.

There was a crystal ashtray on the nightstand.

"—so you see, it's just a means to an end. No hard feelings right?" Christian's words cut through.

He shifted.

It was time.

I bucked up from below doing my best to displace his weight off of me. The knife in his hand clattered to the ground, bouncing a few feet along the hardwood floor.

"You bitch!" He swung his hand, slapping me across the cheek. It was the same side as Stephen had hit me, and I grit my teeth against the added pain.

He rolled off the bed to grab the knife.

It was now or never.

I tugged the rope, one last yank with my fingers before I pulled on my wrist as hard as I could.

The relief was instant as it freed, sliding through the larger hole I had managed to make.

"What are you—" Christian yelled, standing up, knife in hand.

I ignored him. Ignored my racing heart, my sweaty palms, my anxiety.

I couldn't see him as I reached out, latching onto the crystal ashtray with my now free hand. It was *heavy.* I blindly swung it back in his direction.

It made a satisfying crunch as it landed against his nose. I heard a clatter as the knife tumbled to the floor again.

My eyes were on him now. His nose a bloodied mess.

"You stupid fucking bitch!"

I had free rein except for my one wrist still secured to the bed frame. I wasn't going to lay down and wait for him to kill me.

This was my chance.

Adrenaline pumped through my veins, pushing my terror to the very back of my mind.

He wasn't thinking as he launched himself back onto me.

I wrenched my free hand back and smacked the ashtray into him again. This time it landed on a soft spot on the side of his temple. I was aiming for where the gun had hit me earlier, but I couldn't quite reach the spot.

I just wanted to knock him out. To be able to get away from him while I waited for my men.

But he didn't stop; his hands found my throat and he began to squeeze. Pushing me into the mattress.

Black dots marked my vision.

It was harder now, there was less range, but I managed to hit him with the ashtray again.

This time, the move stunned him and I kicked up again. It served to loosen his grip around my neck.

He was still awake. Conscious.

I hit the ashtray against him again.

The noise was a disgusting *squish* as it dug into his head, but I didn't stop. *Couldn't.*

My body separated from my mind.

I closed my eyes and swung again.

I was that girl who was just told her father died.

And again.

Thwap!

I was that teenage girl who was bullied for being different. *Fat.*

And again.

Thwap!

I was that high-school girl lured to the roof by her teacher and nearly raped.

And again.

Thwap!

I was that same high-school girl in love with a man she could never be with.

And again.

Thwap!

I was that woman who was heartbroken after another break-up from another vanilla man.

And again.

Thwap!

I was that woman who was back on that same god forsaken roof with my predator.

And again.

Thwap!

I was myself just hours ago with a dead mom and a father back from the grave.

And again.

Thwap!

I kept hitting him. His brain matter was now gracing the crystal, but I paid it no mind. He wasn't moving, wasn't yelling profanities my way anymore.

I took out decades of buried rage. Of indignation. Of sadness. Of *grief*.

My arm was poised in the air to swing again when cold fingers wrapped around my wrist. I wrenched away and attempted to smack the crystal against the intruder, but another hand stopped me.

"It's okay. We're here."

I was that lost girl again, Oliver's voice cutting through an episode. I opened my eyes, finding his soft blue; a comforting color.

He had saved me from my own mind all those years ago at that cemetery, just as he was doing so now.

The crystal fell from my crimson fingers.

"Ellie."

My attention found Maddox behind him. He was a beacon of light piercing through my turmoil.

"It's okay Ellie. You're safe now."

"Untie her," Emilio snarled out, stepping into the bedroom just behind Maddox. He surveyed the area, his harsh features turning soft as he met my eyes. "You did a good job, Isa."

My men were here. I was safe.

I went to turn my head and look down. To see exactly what I had done, but Oliver finished freeing my wrist and swept me into his arms before I could. He blocked my vision with his hand.

"Take her to the car," Oliver ordered, maneuvering me into Maddox's waiting embrace.

Maddox's calm aura wrapped around me as he quickly left the room. He held me as if I was a newborn. My head rested on one arm as he cradled me.

I loved Oliver and Emilio, but it was with Maddox that I finally could relax. That I knew no matter what, he would keep calm and sane.

"Yara...my dad?" I whispered out hoarsely, watching his face carefully.

Maddox's lips tightened. A crease forming between his eyebrows. "Your dad is safe. Yara is"–his arms flexed, tugging me even closer into his frame–"I won't lie to you. She is hurt *badly.*"

We were walking down a hallway now, and I squirmed against him, wanting to escape, needing to go to her.

"Stay still. She's in the hospital. We found her first. You were taken to a different location. That's why we were so late."

He looked down as he stepped over something.

I followed his attention. A body. It was face up, but I didn't recognize who it was since half of their head was missing.

Maddox covered my eyes as Oliver had, stopping me from taking any more of the carnage in. It wasn't the only body in this hallway.

I found that I didn't even care. My mind focused solely on my friend.

"You need to take me to her!"

Yara had to be all right. I needed to see her. I needed tangible proof that she wasn't going to die. That she would make it through this.

She had to.

"I will, but Ellie"–his voice broke–"please, Ellie. Please don't leave us like that again. This world that Emilio is in isn't safe. I want nothing more than to take you away from both of those men. Neither deserve you."

Maddox finally pushed open a door at the end of the hallway of death, and I blinked my eyes at the onslaught of light.

How much time has passed?

"*Maddox.*" The word came out shaky, raspily. My throat was sore from being nearly strangled to death.

Maddox paused, staring down at me before placing his forehead to mine. His was much cooler than my own, and I welcomed it.

"Don't be mistaken. I am *never* going anywhere. And I won't take you from either of them. I know how much you care about them. How much you love them. And that's okay. You are worth it. I love you. But I need you to be careful. *Please.*"

I reached my hands up to cup his face but paused.

They were covered in a sticky red, something reminiscent of silly putty. "I killed him."

Maddox walked to a vehicle parked on the road. We were on the outskirts of town, the industrial district, and it was the only visible vehicle I could see.

He maneuvered open the door and slid into the backseat, his arms still wrapped around me. "He was going to die one way or another. You simply sped up the process."

"I should feel bad. I should feel distraught."

"You're in shock."

I shook my head laying it against his chest, listening to the steady beat there. "No, Maddox...I think...I think I liked it." As soon as I spoke the words, I knew them to be true.

Maddox placed his chin on the top of my head as the front doors of the vehicle opened.

"To the hospital," Maddox grunted.

"No, we need to take her home," Oliver argued, settling into the driver seat.

"She needs to get looked at anyways. Let her see Yara," Emilio countered, turning in his seat to examine me. "Your neck is already starting to bruise, Isa, but you're going to be okay. You did a good job." He offered me a soft smile which I returned.

"Fine!" Oliver snarled out. A moment later, we were speeding down the road.

The entire time Emilio watched me with his critical intensity. "You're okay with it, aren't you?"

"With what?" I asked, shifting against Maddox.

"She is," Maddox confirmed.

Emilio laughed, a deep husky noise that shot straight through me. "You were meant for us, my Bella Isa. Maybe it's time you two told her about Harry while all the blood and gore is fresh?"

The car swerved before Oliver corrected it.

"You're a fucking asshole," Oliver advised him. He found my eyes in the rearview mirror. "Look Isobel, you have horrible taste in men."

"Ourselves included," Maddox chimed in, squeezing me to him.

I had zero idea where this was headed, but I was preoccupied by my concern for Yara. "Sure," I agreed.

"Well, we hired help to eliminate any worrisome men," Oliver stated matter-of-factly. His eyes narrowed in the mirror.

"Eliminate?" I broke from his stare and glanced at Emilio.

He was turned in his seat, watching me.

"Yes, my Bella Isa. They hired a man named Milo to 'help' them deal with any problems that arose. Did they know I was Milo? No, they didn't." Emilio laughed.

My brain was a sloshy mess of confusion.

"We unknowingly hired Emilio to assist with separating you from the men you dated. Sending a text from, let's say, Hallie's number to Harry," Maddox murmured into my hair.

Ice sliced through my skin. "Why?"

"Why?" Oliver sneered from the front seat. "Because they didn't deserve you if they were going to be that easily swayed. You deserved better. And haven't you realized by now? We're not the 'good' guys, Isobel."

Why did that send jolts of neediness across my nerves? What was wrong with me?

"So, what happened to Harry? Or was that it?" I wasn't even mad. But why were they telling me this all now?

Except, I was almost grateful they were. Layer it onto me now while I'm in shock and then I would process it all later.

And I guess in some way, they *had* done me a favor. If it was that easy for my boyfriends to be swayed...

"I killed him," Emilio shrugged as if he was discussing the weather. "Just killed Hallie too, but she had a role in your step-father's empire. She deserved it, I promise."

He reached a sturdy hand back to cup my cheek.

"That turned you on, didn't it? That I would kill a man for you? You were made for us weren't you?"

I didn't want to admit he was right, so I turned my face into Maddox's chest instead.

This is my life now. This is my life now. This is my life now.

Discussing murder as if it's the weather all while my best friend is in the hospital.

I needed to focus on Yara. On making sure she was okay.

Everything else could wait. I would process it all in my own time.

Emilio chuckled. "Thought so. Now we need to stop to change, but then let's get you to your friend."

Chapter 28

Maddox

His Ellie

It had taken two weeks. Two weeks to finally convince Ellie to come home and sleep in her own bed. That she didn't need to be at Yara's side. That each of them would take a post in her stead.

The first up, much to his chagrin, was Oliver.

Oliver had drawn the literal short straw, had Maddox made them all short with the knowledge Oliver would demand to draw first?

It was a possibility.

But Maddox was aware he wasn't going to be able to play fair in this world. Not with three men vying for Ellie's attention. He had accepted the other two men into her life, hell he found it hot as fuck seeing them with her.

In fact, he had watched through Emilio's camera feed as Oliver had his way with their sleeping girl. Maddox told himself it was to make sure Oliver didn't go too far, and maybe that was partially the truth. But when she had woken up? When Oliver had slammed into her?

Maddox had tugged his own dick out at that point, thrusting into his hand, until he came.

Ellie tossed in her sleep bringing him back to the present. He wasn't going to wake her up, this was the first time she had slept in weeks. She needed it.

They were back in Emilio's house, in their *home*. While Maddox didn't want to admit it, he knew that they would be relocating to Florida. It made the most sense. Ellie's company was easily managed remotely, and they had a crew of employees in New York to do the grunt work necessary to welcome potential new clients.

But Emilio was needed here. He was still cleaning up the mess that Christian and Stephen had caused in their wake. Both men were dead, but they left behind legacies.

They had all but run the Landons from town. Unfortunately, the Yorks were a different matter. While they didn't have any blood relatives left in town, it had only taken a few days for one to arrive.

Simon York. Maddox hadn't met him, but from what he had heard, he seemed a much better man than his predecessor. Only time would tell.

A quick agreement and understanding was formed. Christian had acted on his own volition without his family's backing, so it wasn't hard to put a new treaty in place. Simon agreed and the town was back to its falsity of peace.

The three families, now down to two.

"Maddox," Ellie murmured sleepily, taking his full attention.

For a moment he thought she might still be asleep, but then he felt her small soft hands creeping their way across his skin.

Her fingers traced upwards until they found his scar. Where he had been shot.

"This is where the bullet hit her too. It's the same, so she's going to be okay. She's going to survive it, just like you did," Ellie repeated the line he had heard her say a dozen times before.

That was true, except Yara's situation was a bit different.

"Maddox," Ellie shot up suddenly before rolling over to face him. Even in the dark he found her eyes. "She's pregnant. What if she doesn't make it?

What if her baby doesn't? What if the baby is my sibling? But if her dad is my step-dad and her baby's dad is my dad–does that mean the baby would be both my sibling and my niece or nephew?"

Maddox hadn't been ready for all of that and simply reached out, tugging Ellie onto him. He cupped her face in his bulky hand. "She's going to be okay. The baby is going to be okay. And when all is said and done, you will get all the answers you need and find out if the baby is your sibling or not. But for now? You need to rest, sweetheart. You're vanishing before our eyes. We're worried about you, your bruises are fading, but you haven't talked to us. Told us what happened in that room."

Ellie fell forward onto his chest, he almost expected her to doze off again, but she was watching him instead; observing him. It put him on guard.

What is going through that brilliant brain of hers?

"I need to feel you," she murmured.

That had not been what he expected, but his dick agreed with her sentiment.

She was no longer the woman he had watched for so many years, the one that had been beaten down by the world's judgments. Here in this room, Ellie was the confident, beautiful, self-assured woman that he always knew her to be.

He hoped that she would continue to see how perfect she was, would continue to grow as the years progressed.

She bent down, gripping his hardened dick through his boxers. Tonight, she had fallen asleep in one of his shirts and nothing else. He was hoping he could slowly do away with all of her sleep dresses and replace them with his clothes. They were practically the same after all, but he wasn't going to push the matter.

Yet.

Wet. Warm. Swelling pleasure.

He was so incredibly wrapped in his own mind that the sneaky woman was able to free his dick and swirl her hips onto him.

"Ellie," he loudly growled into the room, the sound reverberating off the walls.

"You know," she hummed, placing her hands on his shoulders and driving him firmly onto the bed.

She lifted before falling down on his length.

Electricity snapped at him all along his skin, to his dick, to his toes, and back up to his balls.

"I found out who else you used to call Ellie."

He stiffened.

"Oliver was mad you played that trick on him to stay at the hospital," Ellie grumbled. "My nickname came from your *dog?*" She jumped off of him, his dick pulling free.

She tried to roll off the bed, but he caught her.

"No, I don't think so. Finish what you started." He shifted to his knees, tugging her ass up. Her juicy fucking ass. "It was my favorite dog." He swatted at her before he slammed back into her primed cunt.

"Fuck!" Her soft lyrical moan empowered Maddox.

He reached forward, rubbing at her clit furiously as he bent over her back. He found her neck.

Maddox had wanted to leave his mark there but wanted to wait for her to heal first.

He used his other hand to grab her gently by the neck to pull her upwards, he met her halfway his mouth latching onto the skin there. Sucking and biting as he went.

Her moan vibrated through his hand, through his mouth, through his dick. She was enveloping every piece of him. He pounded into her aggressively, losing control of his inhibitions, forgetting to dial it back.

He expected her to try to escape, to say her safeword, not to push back on him. Matching every beat he thrust into her.

A guttural noise that stemmed from his chest, left his lips as he unlatched from her neck. A moment later and her cunt clenched around him, the familiar feeling of her orgasming around him.

She screamed as he finished himself, imprinting his mark into her.

His sight blurred as he came deep inside of her, but he didn't pull free. He wanted to fill her, to keep himself deep inside of her. Remind the other two men that they may be a part of her life, but he already owned a part of her too.

"If you two are done, there's a certain woman that has woken up and is asking for you," Emilio's voice cut through the dark.

Maddox knew he had been there, but he realized Ellie might not have when she jumped underneath him.

"You asshole!" she squeaked out, but then his words seemed to land. "Yara?"

Much to Maddox's chagrin, she wriggled off of his cock. He turned back to Emilio baring his teeth in irritation.

Ellie hopped off the bed and Maddox followed the movement. Even in the dim lighting he could make out the mess he had made of her. The marks, his cum glistening between her thighs, her unruly hair.

He was incredibly satisfied, and all of his previous frustration dissolved.

"Go get cleaned up Bella Isa, you're leaking," Emilio stated calmly, only the hint of annoyance saturating his tone.

Ellie lifted a pillow off the bed, launching it in Emilio's direction. Maddox had to contain his laughter as it landed against the man's face.

"Overbearing men!" She stomped off towards the bathroom. "Five minutes and then we're leaving!"

"I love you, Ellie!" Maddox called out to her as she slammed the door shut on them.

He was immensely happy when he heard the soft "I love you too" through it.

"Put some fucking clothes on, I'm tired of staring at your ass." Emilio's tone was rough now, devoid of its previous softness.

Maddox ignored him. He would deal with all the assholes in the world if it meant at the end of it, he would end up with his Ellie.

Chapter 29

Izzy

A dull ache throbbed between my legs as I shouldered open the hospital door to Yara's room. Oliver was already inside, but Emilio and Maddox followed me in.

"Yara!" I screamed, rushing into the room, but before I could get to her, two men stepped into my path.

I recognized Kazi as Emilio's driver but not the other.

"Mateo," Emilio's tone was harsh. "Is this going to be a problem?"

"Yara is my top assignment, all others will be completed as directed," the giant of a man barked out. He was huge, even bigger than Maddox, and I craned my neck to meet his eyes.

"Yara is my best friend," I argued, stretching up to push against the goliath's chest.

He went to protest, but then Yara cut through. "Let her see me you fucking oaf. We talked about this. In fact, everyone out except for Izzy!"

Emilio stepped forward, kissing the top of my hair, squeezing my hand before directing his attention to Kazi and Mateo. "It seems we have some matters to discuss now that she's awake."

They gave him a sharp nod, offering Yara one last look before exiting with everyone.

Now it was just Yara, myself, and my dad in the room.

James sat in the hospital chair. His head was in his hands. He lifted it, offering a sad smile, before shifting to stand.

He and I had talked briefly right after everything had happened. He explained how my mom had taken me and left in the dead of night. Of his fruitless searches in finding me. How Stephen had sought him out. But he didn't dive into Yara–we agreed to wait until she woke up.

"You can stay if you'd like James," Yara offered my dad a simpering smile.

My view of her was now unobstructed, and I finally took her in.

Bruised, battered, but *smiling*. As if this was just another fucking day at the office.

"No, you two need to talk. But Isobella, after, will you find me please?" James stood up, his hand moving on its own to brush away Yara's hair off her face.

He was looking at her with absolute devotion.

I expected to hate it. To get the ick. But I didn't. Yara had been alone for too long, she needed someone. Did I wish it wasn't my dad?

Well duh, but oh fucking well.

After the door shut behind my dad, I turned my full attention to Yara. "So, this is why you didn't want me to call you mamacita?" I chuckled awkwardly, taking the chair my dad had just been sitting in next to her.

She extended over and weakly punched me. "Shut up! You know you're a bitch!?"

"Hey at least this bitch didn't fuck your dad." The joke fell flat between us, and I cringed a bit.

Her face whitened. "I'm sure you heard, but he's dead. Stephen is finally and officially dead. Gone from my life."

I watched her, we had been best friends for over a decade, but we clearly had kept secrets from each other. We both had our own sordid pasts.

"Yara... I'm going to tell you everything now. All of my secrets. Every piece that I have kept hidden from you, and I would love for you to do the same. But you don't have to, you can keep anything you want from me. You know I'll love you no matter what though don't you?"

"I'm ready to listen. I'll be the therapist you never went to, no matter how much I pestered you. Though I guess mine didn't really work. But yeah girl, I think it's time. No more fucking secrets."

"Look what had happened was." I joked, falling back in my chair.

"Shut up, you're such an idiot!" She laughed a bit before coughing. It took her a few moments but eventually she caught her breath.

"You're okay though, aren't you? And the baby? Do you know whose it is? You didn't lose it, did you?" I had not learned the ways of social etiquette and the questions blurted out one after another.

"Nuh uh uh, you first. But yes the baby is healthy, happy, and all that jazz. But everything else, I answer after." She flashed her teeth before settling back on the bed.

I took that as my cue to start.

I wasn't exactly sure where, so I decided to begin with the story of my mother. She had heard bits and pieces before but not the whole of it.

"Your mother was a raging cunt, like god rest her fucking soul. But *fuck!*" Yara exclaimed when I was done with that portion.

She wasn't wrong. I loved my mom, I did, but it was hard to mourn her loss when she had truly been dead to me for years.

I then moved onto my ordeal with Sebastian.

"I'm so sorry I wasn't there." Her voice was thick with emotion.

At the time, she was dealing with her own problems. Daniel, her first boyfriend, had not been kind. He was why I persuaded her to leave town, helped her change her name *again*, how she ended up starting her company.

Next was how Emilio came into play.

"You're fucking married?! And I wasn't invited? I am going to kill that man."

"Maybe don't, you know, since he's my husband and all." That still hadn't fully sunk in. We had been going nonstop since the impromptu "wedding."

I continued on with my story. The sordid pasts of all my men. Another run in with Sebastian. Christian's need for revenge. The *murder* I committed.

She stayed silent through it all.

"Emilio loved you so much he sent a guardian angel to watch over me," Yara eventually chirped up, ignoring my confession altogether.

"What do you mean? And what about the *murder* I committed."

She waved her hand. "He deserved it."

What the fuck? Is murder just the norm now?

I had said I liked killing Christian, and while it had been exhilarating–taking back my power, saving myself–I didn't think I wanted to kill again. But it had healed a piece of me I had tucked so far under a rug I wasn't aware it was there. That it was broken.

"Kazi, he used to be his driver, but Emilio sent him to keep tabs on me." Yara then explained how she had run-ins with Daniel again, stalker style, and her entire ordeal with Kazi and then how Mateo was sent, too.

Finally, she got to the point about my dad.

"I didn't know, but Izzy. I love him. I'm in love with him. All three of them. But that's crazy isn't it?" she whispered, the machine hooked up to her began to beat more rapidly as her heart rate sped up.

"Yeah ... You know that I have my own harem now, I guess. Is this what it's like when you're a boss ass bitch?" I cackled, trying to pull the lightness back into our conversation. "And I'm not mad at you Yara. You didn't know. But as long as you two don't hurt each other. I won't be able to side with either of you."

She carefully sat back up on her hospital bed, her hand finding mine. She met my eyes. "I love you Izzy and I promise not to hurt him. And fuck if he and I don't work out for whatever reason, you're not going to lose me as a best friend. I promise."

I smiled at her. "Agreed. Alright baby cakes, my side is done. Now it's time for you to tell me your story. The whole thing."

"Fuck, alright so it started one night at a comedy club..."

Chapter 30

Izzy

I leaned down to hug Yara carefully. "I'll see you soon," I promised, reeling from everything she had told me. "Get some rest."

My poor best friend had gone through so much, but never again. Not if I could make sure of it.

Stepping into the hallway, my dad stood against the wall.

A sentinel.

For me? Or for *Yara*?

"Do you love her?" I asked, staring into him.

His lips quirked at the corners, the crease between his brow smoothed out, and his eyes softened.

I had my answer.

"I do," he confirmed.

"Okay, I love you dad, but don't hurt her. She deserves the world. And listen...I'm sorry. I'm sorry I believed mom and never looked for you," I rasped out.

"Sweetheart, it wasn't you. And I know you're all grown now, and that this situation is a bit *different*, but I will be here for you from here on out. I won't question your choices, you always did have a strong sense of character. But even still, if you ever need to escape, I can make it happen, no questions asked." He opened his arms for me.

I didn't hesitate, I fell into his familiar embrace. He always smelled like the air after it rained and that was present even now. The nostalgia pulled forth a plethora of memories.

My dad and I had been close before my mother snatched me away. She stole years from us. It was hard to not be angry with her, but she was dead now. I couldn't scream at her, I couldn't question her choices. I simply had to accept it.

For a few moments we just stood like that. "I missed you, too." I sobbed into his shoulder.

And I had. But now that he was here, I felt a piece of myself healing.

"I think a part of me always knew you were alive. I never accepted your death." It was true, it was partially why I never looked for him. I didn't want confirmation he was dead. It felt like I could play pretend without seeing the obituary. But now all I felt was regret.

"I failed you. I should have seen the signs that your mother wasn't mentally stable. I just never expected her to take you from me." He shook as he held me.

We stood like that for a few more moments in silence. Soaking up over a decade of loss, of a thousand missed events. My graduation, my company, my first boyfriend, my *marriage*.

"I got married...to Emilio." I had almost forgotten in the chaos of the last few weeks.

My dad stiffened before dropping his arms around me and stepping back. He reached up, cupping my face carefully. "If he hurts you, I will kill him. Cartel boss or not."

I cracked a smile. "I know."

"Ellie!" Maddox's voice came from my left down the hallway.

"Go join your men. I'll be here when you need me. I'm not going anywhere, and from what Yara has said, it seems we might all be moving here."

On that note, he stepped around me and back into Yara's hospital room.

"Isa," Emilio's voice was a shock as he breathed the name into my ear.

"Isobel," Oliver was next to join our reunion in the hospital.

"Why must you all call me different names?" I exhaled. "My name is Isobella, Izzy for short. Not Ellie, or Isa, or Isobel."

"Is that right? She's being feisty, isn't she?" Emilio cracked out, wrapping his arms around me from behind.

"She is," Oliver agreed. Stepping in front of me a devious expression, darkening his face.

They were crowding me, making me all hot and bothered. I needed to get out of here.

"We're in a hospital! Not a brothel. And when did you two start agreeing on anything?"

Though I was secretly grateful for it; their bickering hadn't been my favorite part of this arrangement.

"You heard her," Maddox grumbled, moving up next to us.

"See the voice of reas—"

"But there's an empty closet down the hallway." Maddox yanked me from between the two men and threw me over his shoulder. "Finders keepers!" He laughed raucously.

"Get back here! Emilio, don't just stand there! Help me get her from him!" Oliver barked out.

Is this what my life is going to be like from here on out?

Emilio caught up, tripping Maddox, but Oliver caught me before I could fall to the ground.

"Mine now!"

"I'm not a football!" I grumbled as I was jostled about.

Oliver spanked my ass before Emilio was there to take me onto his shoulder.

"My *wife!"* He cackled.

"We're going to fix that!"

I could get used to this life.

My face bounced against Emilio's back as he ran and I came to the startling realization.

I didn't think about my weight much anymore. The world's oppressive hand wasn't pushing me into the ground. I wasn't trapped with vanilla men.

I was absurdly and astoundingly happy.

It certainly took me a while and the help of a few men to rebuild my confidence, but I had finally hit a point where I accepted that I may not be everyone's type of beauty.

But I can at least be my own.

Epilogue: Izzy

Three Weeks Later

"I don't want to go on vacation! Yara just got out of the hospital, and I need to be there for her!" I crossed my arms over my chest, staring Emilio down.

The barstool I sat on was the perfect height where I couldn't quite touch the ground. Instead, I kicked my legs against the kitchen island as I continued my pouting.

Emilio turned from the stove, he was in the process of making breakfast. Oliver stood to his left.

"You're going to overcook the eggs." Oliver fully distracted Emilio from responding and gained a spatula in the side for it.

Oliver was still struggling with Emilio, but at this point it was mostly comical to watch them bicker.

Maddox wrapped his bulky arms around me from behind.

"You're home." I sank back against his chest, smiling softly up at him.

"Yes, Ellie. Your employees are all set and have met the new manager you chose. Uh—Susan?"

"Her name is Kathy," I stated smugly. "She was always such a good worker bee, I felt she could handle it."

"She wasn't quite as enthused when I educated her on your part in the company, but she couldn't say no to the package you offered her." Maddox let go to reposition himself before placing something on the bar counter in front of me.

My sparkly stapler and pile of manhwas from my desk.

"You know you're the best, right?"

Oliver broke from his squabble with Emilio. "Hey! I reminded him what items you wanted! How is *he* the best?"

I ignored Oliver, flipping through the manhwa pile instead, leaning to the side into Maddox. "Boss man is mad," I whispered conspiratorially.

"Isobel," Oliver griped. "You can't call me that unless you want me to fuck you before breakfast."

I gasped, mockingly. "Sacrilege!"

Maddox placed a brand-new laptop in front of me next. "Your work is all on this now. Everything you might need and all of the different programs you designed. Emilio backed it up and added extra security precautions."

Oliver grumbled again.

"Oliver ensured all of your clients are on here and suggested the idea," Maddox admitted.

Emilio pushed the laptop to the side carefully and set a plate of food in front of me–eggs, bacon, homestyle potatoes.

My mouth salivated a bit. "You are *all* the best," I corrected myself from earlier before digging in.

Emilio propped against the counter just watching me, but I felt none of the typical self-consciousness.

When I was on the last bite of food, he spoke, "It's our honeymoon."

I choked, and Maddox knocked against my back.

Emilio sighed, glancing between the two men. "Go ahead. I know you have kept them on you."

I set my fork down. Emilio extended out taking my hand, before lightly tugging the band there off.

I was confused until Maddox turned my chair to him, he helped me off the stool, before getting down on one knee, ring box in hand.

"Ellie, nothing in our life is typical, average, or normal, but I wouldn't have it any other way. Would you accept this ring as a token to represent the rest of our lives together?"

My vision blurred as tears formed, the whiplash from the playful to serious almost too much. "You're all going to do this when I just ate, am wearing nothing but a T-shirt, and haven't washed my hair in a week?" I joked before nodding. "Yes, of course I will."

Maddox slid the band into place; it was thin, but uniquely shaped, as if it were missing another part.

He stood up, offering a chaste kiss before Emilio was there to yank me in his direction. He dropped to his knee.

"This time, I want your full consent. Will you be my wife? My person for the rest of our days?"

I jerked my head in agreement. "Do I even have a choice?" I quipped.

"No." He slid the second ring in place, it went perfectly with the first, a soft click sounding as it was secured.

I grew a bit nervous. "Um, guys, did the ring just make a noise?"

Emilio's lips quirked at the corners, his eyes darkening. He stood, kissing my cheek before I was yanked again.

Oliver gracefully landed on one knee, his curls falling forward in disarray.

This time I wasn't sure I wanted the third ring, but Oliver whipped one out without giving me a choice, his long fingers wrapping around my wrist.

"I think you know how I feel about you. I hope you are ready to handle a lifetime of three men vying for your attention and that you're aware there will unfortunately be no escaping our madness." He shoved the third ring into place.

The click this time was clearly audible.

"Explain to her, she is going to panic." Maddox's warmth pressed against my back, his hands trailing forward and securing my wrist in place. "You can take the rings off, but you have to click this button." He showed me on the side. "Each has GPS tracking, and if you take them off, we're pinged an alert."

Why is this explanation turning me on? What is actually wrong with me?

"But what about washing my hands? Showering?"

Oliver stood now staring down at me. His bright eyes at odds with the shadows that enveloped his face. "Then we'll know." He pinched my chin between two long fingers, turning my head side to side. "My vote was for a collar."

I knew without a doubt he wasn't joking and it caused my heart to beat even more aggressively in my chest.

"Now where are we going on our honeymoon?" Emilio cut through the tension.

I closed my eyes, falling further back against Maddox's chest. I knew for a fact that Emilio would have agreed with Oliver, it was most likely Maddox that vetoed the collar idea.

"Somewhere secluded." I heaved a sigh.

There was clearly going to be no escaping this honeymoon, and I could at least bring my work with me.

One Week Later

"Time to take off her blindfold." Emilio's voice stabbed through the darkness.

Being on a plane blind-folded had actually managed to nearly negate my fear of heights. I was hoping it would have dissipated entirely with Sebastian's death, but no such luck. Trauma worked in mysterious and disgusting ways.

Plus, there was the fact they wanted this *honeymoon* to be a surprise.

I blinked rapidly as the darkness was replaced with the very bright glaring sun. For a moment, I thought we might still be in Florida, but then I turned my head side to side, taking in the view.

"When I said secluded–" I spun on my heel to face my three men.

Maddox at least had the decency to look sheepish, but Oliver and Emilio just appeared *smug*.

"I did not mean a fucking private island!"

A week on this private fucking island with my men, *what could possibly go wrong?*

Epilogue: Emilio
His Isa

Six Days Later

Emilio paced outside their bedroom door. Tonight was their last night, and he would be damned if he didn't do what he had been planning.

He went ahead and shed his clothes. Oliver, Maddox, and Isa should all be asleep. He just hoped they stayed that way long enough for him to sink into her cunt.

Emilio did his best to quietly creep into the room, for he knew his precious Isa slept soundly inside. Just as he knew that when she awoke it would be to him. Inside her. Filling her up, fucking her, and fulfilling her darkest desire. *Again*. He might just have to fight off two men in the process.

"She's fast asleep," Maddox murmured through the darkness, the only light coming from the moonlight that shone through the balcony doors. "Oliver is too. You might want to keep it that way with him."

"What if we wake him up with her on him? Do you think he would like that?" Emilio whispered, crawling on the bed.

Maddox had already pulled the blanket off his sleeping beauty.

She was a marvelous sight to take in, and he wondered not for the first time how he had found her. How he was deemed to deserve her.

He didn't, was the answer.

None of them did.

She wasn't wearing her typical sleep dresses that he had found her in all those weeks ago, she was in Maddox's shirt instead.

"Stop taking her fucking Mumus. They're my favorite," Emilio grumbled out. "And help me get this shirt off of her."

His excitement was surpassing new heights. The possibility of being caught. The thought of watching her stretched on all three of their cocks. The warmth and wetness.

He was insatiable. He needed to be inside of her, to bury into her.

Maddox tugged her gently into his lap as they both worked to carefully remove the offending article of clothing, ignoring Oliver entirely.

Emilio stared down at Isa again. At her round pale breasts, the pink nipples pebbled and awaiting his attention. Her full lips that he knew to be soft and yielding. Her legs shifted in her sleep, widening for him, showing off her bare cunt.

For a moment, he thought she might have woken up but then she let out a gentle cute snore.

Did she know he was here? Was she waiting for him?

Maddox trailed his massive hands along her skin, and Emilio watched in fascination as her body moved into his touch. Goosebumps prickled up as he trailed lower and lower until he found her clit.

"I'm going to start while she's still asleep. See how far I can push into her until she wakes up." Emilio's cock jerked at the thought.

To fuck her before she even realized it was him doing so.

Part of him craved that millisecond of terror and then her instant relief. Her mind grasping what her body already knew.

That she was his.

Maddox let out a breath. "It's no wonder she feels safest with me." His words were at odds with how he moved to her cunt, lathering the wetness there before returning to her clit to rub aggressive circles.

Emilio reached down to find her...dripping. He used some for himself, lathering his cock. He could just jerk off and come all over her body but that wouldn't be enough.

He had his mind made up.

He shifted between her legs, ignoring Maddox entirely, albeit grateful for the brutes' help.

His cock touched her entrance.

Just the tip.

He thrust just a bit in, but then she suctioned him. Welcomed him there.

"Cover her mouth."

Maddox listened just in time as Emilio impaled her the rest of the way.

She woke up with a scream, but it was muffled by Maddox's hand.

"Shhh, it's us, we've got you," he whispered hushed praises into her ear.

Emilio pounded into her, forgetting entirely of their plans to let Oliver sleep through it all. He needed his release. That one second of panic when her eyes had opened? Her body taking all of him even as he violently thrusted into her?

It was an oil fire spreading rapidly across his nerves, burning hotter than he had ever felt before. His balls fucking *tingled*. His heart pounded maddeningly.

"I love you, Isa." And he did. She was perfect for him. Made for him.

She moaned, clenching around him as he filled her.

"Who's up next?"

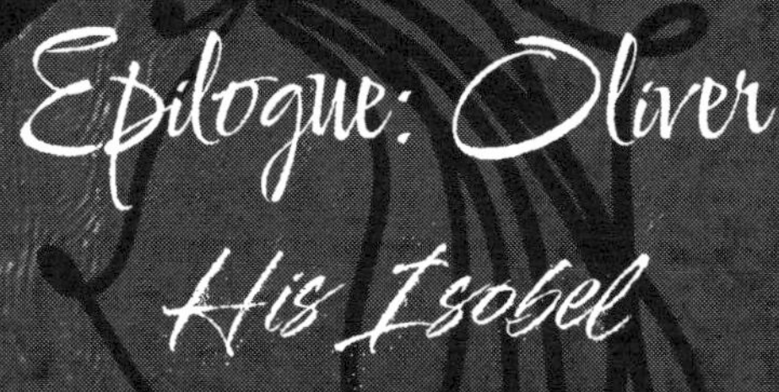

Epilogue: Oliver
His Isobel

That Same Night

Why was this wet dream so realistic?

Oliver shifted in his sleep, his hips thrusting up on their own accord.

"Tell me no if you don't want this," Isobel's voice cut through the dream and he instinctively reached for it.

His hands found the bones of her hips. "Of course I want this, I always want you." And he did. He hadn't had a sex dream this visceral before, but he would take it.

He would fuck Isobel in any plane or dimension as long as it was her on top of him.

And he was certain it was.

Heat. Pleasure. Desire.

Fuck this was too goddamn good.

Was it the vacation that had forced his mind to let go, to relinquish control, and finally relax?

If so, he pledged to do it again and again.

"That's right just like that Ellie, let me sink into that ass of yours."

Except he did *not* want Maddox in his dream.

"Put me in your mouth. Show us how you can take us all at once."

Or Emilio.

Oliver's heart raced against the confines of his chest.

This isn't a dream.

He opened his eyes, lifting his head he took in the full scene.

"Hi there boss man," Isobel said, or at least it sounded like she did. She was on top of him, his dick in her, while Maddox took her from behind.

And Emilio? He was off to the left, her lips suctioned around his cock.

"What the—"

"Just enjoy the ride," Maddox commanded before setting the pace for them all. His hand was on her ass cheeks as he thrust long strokes into Isobel from behind.

Oliver's behind. It was Oliver's ass to take, *not* Maddox's.

He wanted to be angry, but admittedly...

This is fucking hot.

Her taking all of them wasn't something he thought she would do, nor what he had even considered yet. But like this, with her fully stuffed?

Waking up to her on him. Her breasts jiggling in his face as she was driven up and down on his length. His rough fingers digging into her hip bones.

This was *everything*. Better than a hundred blow jobs. A thousand volts of pleasure. A million wet dreams.

Isobel rolled her hips snapping back to meet Maddox.

It was Oliver's undoing.

The desire spilt out of him as he came deep inside of her.

It was only a few more of Maddox's thrusts before he stilled and Oliver felt Isobel clench around him.

He let out a guttural moan. "I see why you like being woken up like that," he growled out as she popped free from Emilio's dick. A trail of saliva falling away.

He didn't hesitate or pause, he reached up and grabbed the back of her head, smashing their lips together.

He ignored the evidence of Emilio and focused on his girl.

On his butterfly.

Once again he was grateful she had kept her wings.

IF YOU DO NOT LIKE PREGNANCY / CHILDREN IN YOUR EPILOGUES DO NOT READ THE REST.

YOU CAN END THE BOOK HERE.

Epilogue: Maddox

His Ellie

Ten Years Later

Maddox sat on the porch of their new home, his Ellie sprawled across his lap. In the background, he heard the playful screams of children.

"Be careful with your cousin!" Ellie shouted, but there wasn't a need.

Oliver was on child duty.

It was funny watching Oliver attempt to corral a herd of children, his hair a mess from the humidity and running around. At least he had help, and Maddox witnessed as Kazi ran across the yard grabbing hold of one of the kiddos.

Maddox squeezed Ellie tighter to him. They had gone through a lot over the years. Highs and lows. Deaths and births. Murder and mayhem. But through it all, Ellie had never lost her spirit, her charm, her *soul*.

"I think this new house is perfect, and now Yara is even closer," Ellie yawned out. The sun splashed across her face, catching in her eyes. She readjusted, moving further into Maddox's embrace.

He welcomed it, he never got tired of her.

"Dad! You have to come play with me!" their oldest, Henry, ran up to them yelling. His caramel eyes left no mistake as to whose DNA he had, but it didn't matter.

He had three fathers. Just like their other three did.

Their youngest, a three-year-old girl, was the only one none of them could agree on. She was the spitting image of Ellie.

"Sure buddy, I'll be right there." Maddox offered an adoring smile before pressing his lips to Ellie's. "You heard him. I'll be back."

Maddox cut his attention to Emilio who was stepping outside. Maddox was grateful when Emilio took his place without a word.

They had fallen into a very amicable friendship. Maddox, Oliver, and Emilio were family at this point. Oliver and Emilio still squabbled occasionally like brothers, but it was never mean-spirited as it had been in the past.

Maddox strode out into the yard, finding Henry at the very far back gate. He walked briskly to him, wondering what had drawn him out there.

"Who's that, son?"

Henry stepped aside.

Simon York and Logan Castillo.

Maddox didn't balk. Perhaps a decade ago he would have, but times had changed. As did the families.

But that was another story, for another day.

"Are the others in the car?" Maddox grinned, opening the gate for them.

Simon held a baby carrier while the other carried the presents.

"Yeah, she's still a bit skittish in crowds, but I think she's going to be okay." Logan cast a worried look back towards the street.

"Here, I'll take the presents, go check on her." Maddox ruffled Henry's hair with his free hand. "Lead the way and then we'll play?"

Henry bobbed his head excitedly, running towards the overflowing presents table.

"I'll wait for them," Simon advised.

Maddox shrugged before turning back to the house. "Suit yourself."

Maddox took in the huge yard as he walked.

Yara was sitting at the bench now with Ellie as they laughed. Emilio acting as Ellie's pillow as she leaned against him.

Oliver played with their remaining three children off to the side with Kazi, Mateo, and...

James. He was holding his youngest.

Maddox was happier than he thought he ever could be.

They had all found unconventional love and maybe it didn't work for everyone.

But it worked for them.

The End...

Hi there!!

You made it to my very first finished story. EVER.

I hope you enjoyed the ride it took you on, but if you're wanting to read more in the Darkest Desires world you can check out Yara's story on Amazon. The first book is OUT and is called: Come Inside.

Also be on the lookout for more in the Darkest Desires universe.

If you want to ~~stalk~~ follow me:

My Facebook group: Sage's Sinners Dark Why Choose

My website: www.sagerelleanne.com

Made in the USA
Columbia, SC
04 July 2025

46b68620-41b8-4dc2-ab4c-bb190544ff1dR01